PRAISE FOR C.P. HOFF

The narrative, which includes occasional black-and-white line drawings by Froese, is, by turns, touching and uproarious—as when Celia puts her hair in pigtails by using a stapler—and Hoff is always ready with well-executed humor: "[Nan] never wears her teeth when she's gardening," Celia tells Old Lady Griggs at one point. "She thinks it's best not to let the plants know her true intentions." The combination of warm nostalgia and a sharp, modern sensibility is perfectly managed, and the promise of future volumes will please readers who want to spend more time in Happy Valley. "— *Kirkus Reviews* (starred review)

ABOUT THE ILLUSTRATOR

Michelle has always had a love for horses and animals that has influenced her artwork since she could first hold a pencil. She first discovered digital art in 2007 and has never looked back since.

She grew up in Brooks, Alberta, and has attended schools in Vancouver, California and Montreal where she has learned how to cultivate her creativity and improve both herself and her craft.

In addition to animals and creatures, she is also inspired by movies, video games and fantasy fiction. She is excited to someday start an independent project where she can illustrate and write full-time.

To see more of her artwork visit www.michelle-froese.com

CANTERBERRY TALES

C. P. HOFF

Illustrated by
MICHELLE FROESE

THE HAPPY VALLEY CHRONICLES
BOOK ONE

All the characters in this book are fictitious, and any resemblance to actual persons, living or dead, is purely coincidental.

Editor - Adrienne Kerr

Copy editor - Elizabeth McLachlan

Cover design - Stuart Bache

Book blurb - Best Page Forward

Copyright © 2021 by C. P. Hoff

All rights reserved.

No part of this book may be reproduced in any form or by any electronic or mechanical means, including information storage and retrieval systems, without written permission from the author, except for the use of brief quotations in a book review.

For my Grandmother
You were so much more

If you like this book, tell a friend, if not, forget you read it.
Black Crow Books

CHAPTER 1

I HAD AN UNUSUAL BIRTHING, more so than any other kid in Happy Valley, but I had competition. On the first day of Grade One, Lenard Hoopenmire said he was born on the hottest day ever recorded in the history of recording hottest days. Bartholomew Dankworth bragged that he was born eleven months after his father died; his mother called it delayed gratification. According to Griggs, though, I surpassed them all, and unlike Lenard and Bartholomew, she's known to be reliable. At the Sunday School Picnic, The Ladies of the Perpetual Indigence Society talked about her dependability. Mrs. Whitford, easily recognized by her beehive hairdo and permanently puckered lips, dipped her spice cake into her black tea and said, "If you want to spread an unpleasantry around town, Griggs is the man to do it."

I wanted to tell her Griggs wasn't a man but knew she'd box my ears for eavesdropping. So, I sat there quietly, concentrating on making my face slack, so she'd think I was a simpleton instead.

"She's reliable enough," Mrs. Whitford continued, looking

about to see who was listening, "to say what others are too scared to or just empty-headed enough to repeat."

The summer I turned seven, Griggs unburdened most of her empty-headedness on me. That was the year my Nan took an out-of-the-house job, spending her mornings stocking shelves at the Happy Valley Druggist; her afternoons she kept for taking in laundry, washing the dainties of the masses, while I handed her the clothespins and spritzed as she ironed. I overheard her telling Old Lady Griggs about it.

"Those new washing machines are a marvel," Griggs said, nudging her chair closer to Nan's kitchen table. "If I had the money I'd buy one myself."

Nan set down the teapot. "It would save time," she said, taking a seat of her own. "But they do seem a bit revolutionary."

"Good God, they're talking about putting a man on the moon. If they can do that they can certainly make an automatic washing machine."

"I suppose." Nan took a sip of her tea.

Nan and Griggs went on about laundering and how far things had advanced, from beating clothes on riverbank rocks to wringer washers. Nan said that now that some of the better-thans had purchased their newfangled machines, they would no longer need her. She seemed disappointed, like she was already missing her raw hands and the scrubbing she'd have to do while ferreting out stains from their unmentionables. She said it was only a matter of time until my spritzing days were done. My heart dropped. Spritzing was one of my favourite responsibilities. If I held the bottle just so, flicked my wrist, I could spritz both the garment and Nan in one fell swoop.

Nan's change in schedule meant she needed someone to mind me in the mornings, and the only someone she could find who was willing was Old Lady Griggs. That was no mean feat, as the ladies at the Sunday School Picnic said, because on most days Griggs couldn't even mind her own business.

It wasn't until the next morning, after the washing-machine conversation, that Nan informed me of her intentions. "Celia, Mrs. Griggs is going to look after you today."

"Yes, ma'am."

"And I want you to listen to her like we were in church listening to a sermon about Jesus. And not your squiggly kind of listening."

That would be hard. On most Sundays I was convinced two ants and a spider were mapping the topography of my body. Their tickling legs wandering in and out of unseen places, every so often stopping to confer with each other. The spider seemed to be the more inept of the three, causing the ants to throw up their little ant arms in frustration. They wished they'd never brought him along. I didn't blame them; spiders make the worst cartographers. The more I thought, the more I wriggled. I could feel each of their tiny feet, some in shoes, the spider in clompy cowboy boots, leaving minuscule bruises all over my delicate skin. I randomly swatted myself to rid myself of my pests.

"Honestly," Nan would groan, and then send me early for Sunday School. Just like she was sending me to Griggs now.

I narrowed my eyes and looked her square in the face. "Old Lady Griggs is nothing like Jesus. She's all, 'don't do this and don't do that.'" I flapped my hands about, mimicking Griggs and her bony ways. "And in Sunday School, when kids get bored and squirm, she makes stuff up." My brow scrunched up without me telling it to. "I saw her pick up an upside-down Bible, flip it open, and without even looking pretend to read 'suffer the little children.'"

"She didn't make that up. The Bible does say that."

"Then she hits us. And we hadn't even said anything about her lazy eye!"

Nan leaned closer, and her voice was as sharp as the church bell. "Today there will be no hitting if you mind her." She wagged a finger. "And call her Mrs. Griggs. Can you do that?"

I shrugged. "That would take the fun out of going."

Nan pointed to my white Sunday School shoes, and I dropped to the floor to put them on.

"Do you want folks to think you're impolite and insolent? That I haven't raised you better than that?"

I didn't know how to respond. Why would I care about being polite or insolent? I was *precocious*, that was what Miss Dobbs, my first-grade teacher said when she wasn't glaring at me and grinding her teeth. In my mind, precocious was far better than polite. There was no joy in being polite. The word plopped out of my mouth like a fresh road apple. I'd rather put on my pinchy church shoes on weekdays than be polite. "All right," I said, doing up my buckles. "I'll try, but I can't promise. 'Old Lady' just slips out when I'm not looking, and I don't think Jesus would mind, because he knows it's the name that suits her best."

Griggs lived three doors down from my Nan and me, just behind a line of overgrown caraganas. I Frankenstein-walked the whole way there, taking the dirt path next to the sidewalk. My arms were straight out in front of me, my lame Frankenstein leg dragging behind, raising a trail of dust. I twisted my bolty neck at a jaunty angle, making it awkward to close my mouth or swallow. If it weren't for the bug I breathed in, I'm sure the line of drool would have reached down to my chin.

Nan scowled as she wiped away my spittle with her freshly pressed hanky. "Remember what we talked about?"

I nodded.

"Good," she said as she nudged me through the Griggs' open screen door and hurried off to work.

I blinked a couple of times before I could make out the kitchen. The place wasn't as bad as I'd thought. I might have called it homey if not for the mothball smell, but the smell was to be expected, considering Griggs kept a life-sized figure of her dead husband sitting at the kitchen table. She claimed it was easier to serve him coffee there than lugging the perc all the way down to the Happy Valley Graveyard.

I had to admit he looked awful friendly in his overalls and checkered shirt. His button eyes were sewn to a nylon stocking stuffed with a mixture of cotton and mothballs. The way he leaned on the table was comforting, as if he was about to say something, or smell one of Old Lady Griggs' stale biscuits. It was hard to believe Griggs could have married such an attractive man. I was about to poke him when Griggs called me from the living room.

I tiptoed toward the voice, and scooched up next to her on her plastic-covered chesterfield.

"Celia, I've got something to show you, but you can't tell your grandmother. She'd skin me alive."

I looked Griggs up and down; I didn't think it'd matter. She wouldn't look any worse skinned than she did now, and I thought of telling her so, but we'd never shared a secret before. She'd never even called me Celia. It was usually *come over here* or *get off of that*. The thought of her using my real name, or letting me touch something without gloves on, made me quiver inside. I nodded and crossed my heart. I would've promised almost anything to see what she was willing to risk her wrinkled hide for. She paused a moment as if she didn't think my heart crossing was bona fide, so I crossed it again. That seemed to satisfy her, because she reached underneath her chesterfield and pulled out a book bigger than the library dictionary, the one Griggs had modified. She'd spent a whole afternoon looking up ungodly words and gluing their pages together. No one uses that dictionary anymore; Nan calls it a monument to stupidity.

"I bought this when you were born," Griggs said, her lazy

eye on me and her ambitious one on the cover. "Thought since the Dionne quints had run their course, it was time for a new face. There has been reason to hope over the years. The whole town kept their eyes peeled for the usual stuff —locusts, floods, spontaneous combustion —we were all very diligent. Mrs. Hempel delivered cross-eyed triplets but there was nothing to raise an eyebrow there, given that family line. Something as simple as a two-headed calf could've replaced them. But you, you were different.

"Once your mother had her first contraction, you were on everyone's mind. It couldn't be helped. With your lineage everyone knew things wouldn't go well." She paused and waggled her eyebrows. "If there was a scandal to be had, or a con to be played, your folks were the ones to do it. You weren't quite as appealing as the Dionnes, but then again who is? Five identical girls in pigtails and pinafores. They were all the rage when I was a girl. Made their town a fortune. So it follows that the one awkward child of freaks could bring in a pretty penny for Happy Valley." Griggs placed a hand on her chest. "I was one of the first to see it. 'She's the ticket,' I said. And the whole town agreed. In fact Oswald Elliot was hired fresh out of high school for that very purpose."

"What purpose?" was the question I asked out loud, but the one bouncing around in my head was about parents I'd never met, parents that Griggs had called 'freaks'.

"To document your life, silly. That and painting the gold stars on Main Street. Oswald paints one star for each strip he's made. I'm sure you've seen them."

I nodded.

"Well each of those shiny devils corresponds to what I've been pasting. The hope was that they'd attract outsiders. Folks with pockets brimming with cash so they could have their picture taken in the very spot where Celia Canterberry did this or Celia Canterberry did that. So far it's been a bit of a bust."

I had no idea what she was talking about. I'd never heard of a Dionne quint or an Oswald Elliot. And Nan never talked about my parents or my birth, not even when I pestered her while she was making supper. "Honestly Celia," she'd said, kneading biscuit dough, "I don't know what to tell you."

"I just want to know how I got here."

"The same way we all got here." She wiped her hands on her apron and tilted my chin up with the tip of her flour-dusted finger. "There are regular families," she said, "and then there are families of the heart. We are that kind of family. How we got together isn't important, what is important is that we are."

Before I could pester further, she'd close her eyes and start counting to ten. When she opened them and I was still there she'd make me do chores, like shoe straightening or pillow fluffing. It really wasn't worth standing around to find out which.

Griggs sniffed loudly, bringing my attention back to the matter at hand. "Been pasting every newspaper article about you since. At one time, the local rag was quite frivolous. They covered everything from a new litter of puppies to the best pie at the church potluck. Made it between the pages a time or two myself before I married Mr. Griggs." She puffed up like she'd met the Queen. "Fellas around town used to hold weekly pools to see if there were any takers for my hand in marriage. A picture of me in my Sunday finest and below it, two columns; one for the men who would rather die and one for those who were willing to risk it all." Her voice grew sweet. "Mr. Griggs was in the *willing to risk it all* column." Griggs' sweetness turned sour. "Now, unless you bake a pie that results in a suspicious death, it's no use even trying to make it into print."

I wanted to comfort her by saying, 'and look where that got

Mr. Griggs, all stuffed and fluffed with a nylon stocking for a head,' but decided against it.

"After you were born," Griggs continued, "those feats lost their lustre, and whole pages were devoted to you and your inauspicious birth."

She paused as if proud to know words such as lustre and inauspicious. I wasn't impressed; Nan was stretching Griggs' vocabulary with the Dictionary Game. I could spell inauspicious before I was three; could spell it for her now, if she wanted me to. If I got it wrong, Griggs would never know. She was the worst speller in Happy Valley. Griggs even bragged that at the bank, she'd been told more than once that Griggs had three g's. Never seemed to bother her. She'd laugh and say it was easy to forget when you had a name so fancy. Claimed she didn't want to be showy.

Griggs tapped the scrapbook with a jagged fingernail. "And all those articles, each and every one, they're all right here."

I squinted at the powdery black cover. Little bits of yellowed paper poked between at least half the pages. "Nan never shows me anything from the newspaper. She says it's trash and won't allow it in the house."

"That doesn't surprise me." She thinned her lips until they were hardly more than a pencil line. "It's not very flattering." Old Lady Griggs patted the cover once more like she was reassuring herself. "But I think you need to know all that woman has sacrificed for you. She has the patience of Job, and everyone knows how that turned out."

I tapped my chin. Job. That name sounded vaguely familiar, and I wanted to say who's Job, but thought better of it. Me not knowing someone everybody else knew would only make me look ignorant. Besides, I didn't want Griggs to change her mind and shove that big black book back under the chesterfield.

Griggs lifted the cover to reveal the first page, a mixture of cartoon drawings and strips of cut-out newspaper articles. "That's you," she said, pointing at a cartoon baby held up by a cartoon nurse. "I coloured your face myself. Thought the red cheeks would enhance the cartoon screaming."

I looked at the drawings, whole rows of them, and felt a little disappointed. "Aren't there any real pictures?"

Old Lady Griggs snorted. "There should have been, but Oswald Elliot, that dunderhead, dropped and broke the Happy Valley Journal's only camera, and just a month after they'd hired him! They bought another one, and he dropped and broke it the month after that. Can you imagine?"

I gasped.

"I know! But it didn't matter; he couldn't snap a good picture if his life depended on it. He was so shaky at the prospect of taking the ideal shot that he cut off the heads of most images he took. Folks got tired of guessing who was who by the size of their girth, or the brand of their shoes. He draws everything now, and I must say he's pretty good with a set of freshly sharpened pencils. He's hoping to win a Pulitzer Surprise some day."

"What's the surprise?"

Old Lady Griggs groaned as if she had never been more exasperated in her life. She turned her head so her ambitious eye took in the whole of me. "How am I supposed to know? It's a surprise."

I didn't care about Oswald Elliot and his freshly sharpened pencils. The bald squalling baby with the crayon-coloured cheeks had my full attention. Those cheeks looked like they had hellfire in them, and made me a bit uncomfortable. I pointed at the strip. "Who are all the other cartoon people?"

"Well," said Griggs taking her glasses from her apron pocket. "That's the doctor, there are the nurses, and that woman in the hospital bed, sorry to say, that's your mother."

My heart thumped in my chest. I'd never seen a picture of my mother before, never knew there was one. The first day of school all the kids in my class were asked to draw pictures of their families. In my family, me and Nan were the only ones with faces. My mother and father were big round heads. Oswald Elliot had drawn my mother like she brushed her hair with a tree branch and lived in a cave. "Are you sure? She looks kind of cranky."

"Well, she just had you." Old Lady Griggs licked a fingertip and was about to turn the page.

"What about him?" I pointed to a man in another cartoon box, leaning against a truck outside the hospital.

"That's your father."

"My father," I whispered, leaning closer. I'd never seen him either.

Old Lady Griggs looked from me to the book. "Maybe I should start from the beginning." She cleared her throat and her voice became all fancy, like her nose was pinched so tight it was hard to draw a breath. "As you know, you had an unusual birthing. Not because you were pulled out of any doctor's bag, and not for any ridiculous stork-like reason either. What kind of dim-witted child ever believed that? No, it was unusual because you were born to your grandmother. Sure, your should-have-been-ma was there for the first part, the easiest part. That couldn't be helped. It was her time, and she had to push you out; but as your grandma says, having a child goes far beyond the pushing."

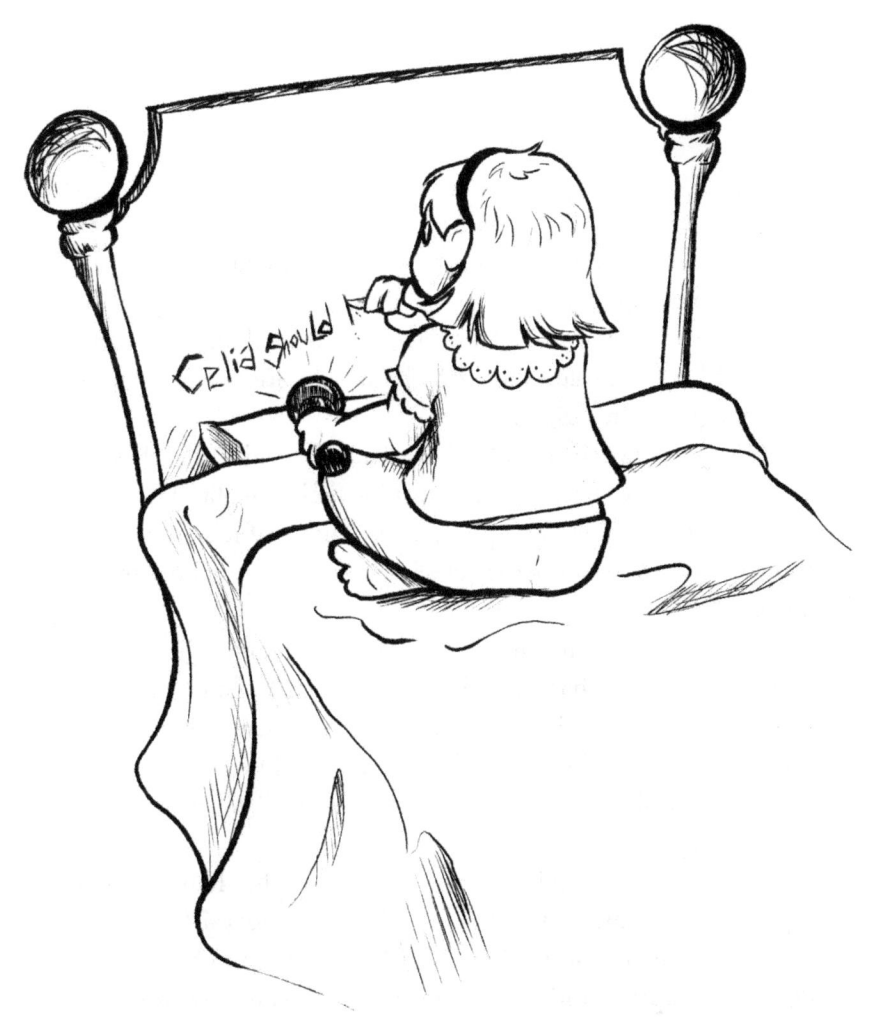

CHAPTER 2

OLD LADY GRIGGS and I were so wrapped up with my should-have-been parents that we didn't notice Nan open the screen door. She was halfway across the kitchen before the sound of her hard-soled shoes caught our attention. I didn't even hear her greet Mr. Griggs.

Old Lady Griggs shoved the scrapbook under the chesterfield and settled back on the cushion lickety-split. Her face turned greeny-white. She squeezed my hand as if it were the last thing she would ever do, the act of someone about to be skinned alive.

Nan walked into the living room. At first, she looked relieved that we hadn't killed one another, but then she frowned. The television was off, and there were no games or toys lying around. She took a deep breath, and her paisley dress expanded until it nearly filled the doorframe. "What have you two been up to?"

Griggs' lazy eye wobbled, and Nan placed her hands on her hips. No one said a word. I could almost hear Mr. Griggs gasping for air in the kitchen. Old Lady Griggs tightened the ties of her apron until they dug into her scarecrow frame. I didn't know if she was readying for a fight, or to run for the hills, but whatever it was she and Nan didn't take their eyes off one another.

I looked from Griggs to Nan and said the only thing that came to mind. "We were cuddling."

"Cuddling? All morning?" Nan sounded suspicious.

"Yup. Except for the times we were singing. Old Lady Griggs does parts."

Griggs nodded like her head was unhinged.

I got up and bowed slightly at the waist. "Thanks Griggs, I've had a lovely time." Then I slipped my hand into Nan's and tugged her toward the door. "See? I even remembered my manners. No one's going to be able to call me impolite or insolent. It almost makes me sad inside."

Nan didn't say anything, just held Griggs in a steely gaze. We tug-of-warred all the way through the kitchen, Nan's gaze fixed on that wobbling eye.

"Where were you?" I asked as loud as I could without yelling.

"I was at work."

"Oh, yeah. I forgot."

"That's understandable," Nan snorted, "with all the cuddling and singing." She didn't say anything more about me and Griggs, but that didn't stop my stomach from flip-flopping every time she glanced in my direction.

Later, at supper, Nan pushed her peas from one side of her plate to the other, tapping her fork after each pass. She looked a little flummoxed. I knew the feeling. Nan called me flummoxed sometimes when I came home from school. At first, I thought it meant I was plugged up and would never be able to go number two again. I'd slowly fill up with all kinds of foul smells and muck until I vomited. But Nan said flummoxed meant stumped, that I wasn't quite sure what was going on. It was a relief.

Sitting at the supper table, she was so flummoxed she didn't notice me making my mashed potatoes into a snowman and pelting it with my boiled peas. I guess the thought of Old Lady Griggs hugging me instead of poking me full of pins seemed highly unlikely. I knew she wanted to talk about it, ask me if Griggs had broken my ribs, if I needed to see a doctor, but couldn't bring herself to wake the sleeping dog that lay between us. I couldn't just sit there, so I kicked the snoozing canine.

"Nan," I said, swinging my legs and smiling. "Aren't you going to talk to me?"

The fork scraped across her plate.

"Nan?"

"I'm tired."

"Too tired to talk? You're never too tired to talk."

"I've never had two jobs before."

"Are you too tired to play the Dictionary Game?"

We played the Dictionary Game almost every night after supper. She'd say a word and use it in a sentence, then I'd repeat it and use another word with a similar meaning. We'd continue that way until one of us ran out of words. It was usually me. Nan claimed a well-honed vocabulary would set some of my naysayers on the back foot. I'm not exactly sure what she meant by that, but it sounded ominous.

"Too tired for even that." She pushed the last of her peas onto her fork. "You like going to Mrs. Griggs?"

I looked down at my mashed potato snowman. He was sticking out his tomato tongue, kind of taunting. I poked him with my fork. "She's not as nice as her husband, but that's not a fair comparison, him being dead. If I close my eyes real tight and only let in a sliver of light she kind of looks like an iguana."

"And you like that?"

I thought my answer had been self-explanatory. "Who wouldn't want to be babysat by an iguana?"

Nan looked pacified and she didn't bring up Griggs again. But I knew she was thinking about her; it was in the way she tapped her fingers on the table, kind of niggling. Nan's eyes held the same look of disbelief they had in Griggs' living room doorway. And no matter what I did, the look stayed there for the rest of the evening.

That night, when I went to bed, I carved 'Celia Should Have Been' into my headboard with Nan's best butter knife. When I finished, the words were hard to make out, all jiggity and jaggity, but when I looked closer, I swear they could have been scratched in there by some midnight killer. The thought made my heart pound. I slipped my flashlight under my pillow, in case the maniac came back; I could conk him on the head. The next morning, I told Nan that butter knives aren't the best carvers; they scare small children. She said I should write the manufacturer so that they could put a warning label on the box. I hated it when she mocked me.

CHAPTER 3

I WAS UP EARLY WAITING for Nan at the breakfast table. She came into the kitchen yawning and stretching, but when she saw me she stood stock still, frozen like a statue in her Fortrell pantsuit. It was an outfit she'd got from the second-hand store two counties over, just to avoid The Ladies of the Perpetual Indigence Society. She wouldn't have been caught dead in any of their castoffs. Nan called them the PIS Ladies behind their backs, and whenever she saw them coming she'd say, 'Elbows out Celia, there be harpies.' Nan looked at my new 'do' with puzzlement.

"What have you done to your hair?"

I patted the top of my head. "Put it in pigtails."

"How?" She came closer and peered at my head.

"With your stapler." I leaned over so she could have a better look. "I thought if I stapled the elastic bands right to my hair," I pulled at a bright pink elastic, "they won't slip out, and I won't have to comb it for a week."

Nan's face went slack like mine did when I pretended to be a simpleton. "Good God, child, you'll be the death of me."

Even though Nan didn't warm to my hairdo right away,

she let me go to Griggs the way I was; she didn't have time to fix it or she'd be late for work. Griggs was waiting for us on her back step, wearing a shabby old pink housecoat with a bare splotch in the back, like she'd been scratching her bony rump on the refrigerator, and her hair was in brown-grey curlers. "Not very promising," I whispered to Nan as we approached.

Nan looked down at me and frowned. "Matches your hair."

Ignoring the jibe, I asked, "With all that bottom-scratching, do you think she has worms?"

Nan twisted her lips as if she were considering the situation. "I don't know, but I dare you to ask."

I was still trying to figure out if Nan was serious when Griggs grabbed me by the arm and shooed me into the house. Through the screen door I could see Nan give Griggs a tight smile. I knew the misgivings she'd had the day before were brewing and bubbling up inside her, biding their time. A witch's brew if ever there was one.

"Don't even bother with your child-rearing lectures, Molly Canterberry. I know the drill," Griggs snapped. "And I'll have you know that just because I didn't have children of my own doesn't mean I don't know what's best for them. I've read Dr. Seuss."

"I think you mean Dr. Spock."

"A doctor is a doctor, smarty pants," she said indignantly, shutting and locking the inside door. If Nan answered back, I didn't hear her.

I stood there for a while looking up at Griggs, not sure if I should run back to Nan or cleave to Griggs and the secrets she had hidden in that black scrapbook of hers.

"We have so much to talk about," Griggs whispered in my ear, the pokes from her curlers jabbing into my cheek. She whisked me through the kitchen and we were back on the chesterfield with the scrapbook before I had a chance to say good morning to Mr. Griggs.

"Where were we?" she asked, slapping the cover with both hands.

"On my should-have-beens," I said, looking around the room at the pots and pans strewn about the floor.

"Never you mind those," Griggs said about the cookware. "In case your Nan sneaks up on us again, we can say we're in a band."

"A pot and pan band!" I said excitedly. "Nan doesn't encourage my musical aspirations."

"I'm not surprised," Griggs said, "I've often told that woman you are rather one-note." Her ambitious eye winked at me. "But let's get back to business, shall we?" She flipped open the scrapbook. "Oh yes, your should-have-been pa."

Me and Old Lady Griggs spent the rest of the morning scouring the first few pages. She fixed her lazy eye on me while her ambitious one scanned the paper. If it wasn't for my curiosity, I might have found it alarming, the way her eyes could fix on two different things at the same time. It would have been all right if I were twins, but I was an only child and I found it unnerving.

The more pages we examined, the more I didn't care that the back of my legs were sticking to her plastic-covered chesterfield, nor how much it would sting when I had to tear them free. I was too busy marvelling at the fact my life had become a comic book story. I was cartoon famous!

"Your should-have-been-pa wasn't any better than your should-have-been ma." Her knobby finger jabbed at a frame. "Look at him in all his miserable splendour, drawn and coloured. He waited outside the hospital throwing stones against her window. That man never even bothered to turn off his rust-bucket truck. Wasteful, that's all I can say." Just thinking about his leaning all casual and lanky in that parking lot seemed to irk her to the quick. "He was a ne'er-do-well, that one."

"Ne'er-do-well," I mouthed back. "Sounds French."

"What the hell are you talking about?"

I shrugged. It didn't matter to me what his last name was. I was more interested in the drawings that Griggs had tinted with her pencil crayons.

"He leaned against that rusty old truck," she said, "smoking and drinking, music blaring out of its crackling old radio like he was having his own personal soiree. Every so often he'd yell, 'Hurry up, woman,' as if she was in some change room trying on a new dress. The whole town talked about it for weeks."

I traced the outline of the truck with the tip of my finger. "What did my should-have-been-ma do?"

"Well, that's where the story gets interesting." Old Lady Griggs licked a finger and turned the page.

It looked like Griggs had spent the better part of an evening colouring the headline she had pasted front and centre at the top of the next page; it contained almost every colour of the rainbow. When she read the words, it was like she had a trumpet in one hand and a scroll in the other. *Illegitimate or Not, A Child is Born.*

I wasn't sure how to take that declaration. Pasted below it were rows of comic strips. Griggs read all the caption boxes and speech bubbles to me, taking her time to do the voices. She said she added the theatrics for my listening pleasure.

In the first row of boxes, my should-have-been-ma was all ragged looking with her mouth gaping open as if she were howling at the moon. Old Lady Griggs said she was the villain. High-cheeked-boned nurses in their crisp white caps and uniforms were the heroines. I could tell because some strange hospital hallway wind tussled their hair about, all lovely and dramatic-like. Beneath them Oswald Elliot had written: *The*

Virtuous nurses, those unfortunate lambs, try to decide what to do next. They whisper and bleat to one another, for the fate of a young life depends on their next move.

Griggs looked up from the strip. "If they could have taken care of your should-have-been-ma's needs through a closed door, I'm sure they would have. They are the bravest nurses I've ever seen. Not that I've witnessed any of their heroics in person, mind you. Just seeing them in the funny-papers makes my heart swell with civic pride."

I wasn't sure about swelling pride. More like bloated embarrassment. Had the whole town read about my ignoble birth? Looking at Oswald Elliot's drawings, I couldn't believe no one had shown them to me before. At least now I understood why Nan hated letting me out of her sight. Without saying a word, I pointed to the next box. Griggs nodded and continued reading. So there would be no mistaking what kind of people I'd come from, she used awful, malevolent voices for their speech. "There," Griggs pointed at the strip. "That's where your should-have-been-pa hollered for your should-have-been-ma to hurry up."

"She looks fired up, as if he'd put a snake in her coffee cup."

"She was, and honestly, who could blame her? Some men should be taken out and shot." Griggs' lazy eye widened, and I wondered about her aim. I wanted to ask her but knew she'd flick me in the head with one of her scarecrow fingers. My head hurt just thinking about it. The nerve of that woman, phantom-flicking me for almost-asking a question. It made me kind of angry inside.

Griggs must have noticed my lack of attention because she slapped the book shut. "I'm preparing to orate," she said, as indignant as if she had caught me rifling through her baggy-bottomed underwear drawer. Old Lady Griggs cleared her throat and re-opened the scrapbook. She tapped the next frame.

With her hair matted to her forehead, our wayward villainess grunts and groans. Between contractions she climbs out of her hospital bed and staggers to the window. "Keep your pants on, fool. If you'd done that in the first place we wouldn't be here now, would we?"

Her partner in crime, stationed in the parking lot below, takes another swig from his bottle and an extra hard pull on his cigarette. He blows big puffs of blue smoke while the banshee hollers.

The commotion is heard all the way to City Hall where Mayor Forde, God-appointed, is holding a town meeting. All the regulars are there: the butcher, the baker, the grocer. They're in the middle of their second hand of five card stud when a screech of agony disturbs their peaceful repose.

"What the hell?" Mayor Forde slams a closed fist against the table. "Can't a man get a moment's peace? Agnes, call that no-good contractor, and ask him if these walls are made of paper." A purple vein pulses in his temple. It is not the first time Mayor Forde questions his own wisdom at deciding to locate Happy Valley's City Hall next to the Happy Valley Hospital, and insisting his brother-in-law, newly released from the Happy Valley Correctional Centre, handle the construction. He suspects that his brother-in-law is scavenging other construction sites to keep costs low, and his advice that a few castoff rose bushes and a bunch of discounted tulip bulbs from the local hardware store will make a soundproof barrier as good as any berm devised by city slickers has been proven false.

"He's skipped bail," Agnes calls back, sticking her chewing gum under the lip of her desk in the outer office. "Your sister is real upset. Says she's knocked up again and she needs you to pick up milk."

Mayor Forde grunts. "Should've saw it coming. That woman's always out of something. Brains mostly." He sucks his teeth. "I'll have to devise another plan." Without looking up from the cards on his protruding belly he hollers, "Agnes, do something about that god-awful racket."

Agnes, sporting her floppy bedroom slippers, shuffles into the mayor's office, an unlit cigarette dangling from her parched lips. She glances into the mayor's hand, and rolls her eyes before she shuffles past and shuts the window.

"God damn it, Agnes, if I wanted the window shut I could've done it myself. Phone down to the hospital and see if someone's having their legs ripped off. If it's someone important, I should be there to give my condolences." He looks up from his hand and smiles at his compatriots. "Got to show my concern for the community."

"I think that's admirable," says the butcher.

"Not more than I do," says the baker, as if to up the ante.

The grocer licks a thick finger of one hand and smooths down the last three strands of his hair. "But I'm the only one who salutes you for it," he says, without bringing his hand to his brow.

"Nan doesn't think so," I interrupted. "She says Mayor Forde should be taken out and shot. She said if that's what God wants for our mayor, that he should be taken out and shot as well."

Old Lady Griggs pulled a bobby pin from one of her hair curlers and started cleaning out the wax from her ears with its rounded end. "I know," she said, as she examined the lump of yellow. "If I had a gun I'd do it myself, not the God part, mind you, the Mayor Forde part. God doesn't sit still long enough to draw a bead." She wiped the pin off on her shabby pink housecoat before reinserting it into the curler. "But there are those that would agree with the mayor. They think if it made it into the paper it must be true. That's the power of the pen."

I was pretty sure Griggs didn't have a clue what she was talking about. Power of the pen sounded like something she had read in the Readers Digest; an article squeezed between Quotable Quotes and Laughter, the Best Medicine. Old Lady Griggs said the Queen of England read the Readers Digest, that's what made her so stately, and since Griggs was such a good royal subject she'd devoted many hours to doing the same thing. I nodded my head just to be amiable and pointed back to the comic strip. "You left off here," I said.

Agnes shuffles out of the room to reapply her lipstick before phoning the hospital.

When another screech disturbs Mayor Forde's peaceful repose, he throws his cards across the table. "Do I have to do everything myself?" *The back of his neck reddens.* "Agnes, get a hold of Doc Marley and ask him if anyone needs to be put out of their misery."

Meanwhile, back in the hospital, Nurse Timmer with a trembling hand returns the telephone to its cradle. "On order of the mayor, I've sent for Doc Marley," *she says, staring at the door of the should-have-been ma's hospital room.*

Nurse Timmer takes the head, while wizened old Nurse Todd takes the tail, their hair blowing free from their caps, almost obscuring their vision. The should-have-been ma lets out a string of expletives that make the angels weep.

"I don't think that language is appropriate," Nurse Todd says, frowning.

"Who asked you?" the should-have-been spits, her eyes wild.

Nurse Todd is flummoxed.

I touch Griggs on the arm. "That means that she can still go to the bathroom."

"Who?"

"Nurse Todd. Flummoxed doesn't mean she's plugged up."

"I know that," Griggs snapped.

I shrugged a little. "I wasn't sure. I just found out myself."

"You keep interrupting my favourite part. Do you hear me?

My favourite part. The part where Nurse Todd gets her comeuppance." Griggs cleared her throat. *Nurse Todd is flummoxed. She stutters and dabs her perspiring forehead with a face cloth while the should-have-been shouts, "Oh, shut the hell up. All your damned stammering is giving me a headache."* She shoots a hairy leg from under the crisp white sheet, almost kicking the unsuspecting Nurse Todd in the stomach.

Old Lady Griggs paused and turned, looked right at me with her ambitious eye. "I don't know if I've said it before, but the good Catholics gasped at the words *damned* and *hell* in bold-faced print, and refused to read the newspaper on Sundays. Lucky for us, they don't know what *knocked up* means. The fun Catholics do, but they just laugh."

"What does knocked up mean?"

"You're not Catholic so I'm not telling you. But I will say that when Doc Marley arrived, he told Oswald Elliot he was surprised your should-have-been-ma's head didn't spin around like some kind of poltergeist. He said with all the bellowing and carrying on he couldn't hear himself think, so he opened his black doctor's bag and showed the patient his bone saw.

"Your should-have-been-ma wasn't any happier to see him than he was to see her. It says right here, it says, *"What the hell is he doing here?"* the should-have-been demands, grabbing hold of Nurse Timmer's collar and pulling her close. *"I never asked for a goddamned doctor."*

Nurse Timmer peels away the should-have-been's fingers one at a time and offers her an assortment of pills. "It's okay," Nurse Timmer soothes her. "Nurse Todd has taken some herself." Nurse Todd stands in the corner smiling, silently rocking back and forth.

The last thing the mayor hears is, "I'm no goddamned horse, and you're not putting me in no bulls##t stirrups." It is the first time Doc Marley delivers a baby from across the room.

I sat there blinky-eyed with my mouth open. Stirrups? No wonder Nan didn't talk about my beginnings. No wonder kids at school ran when they saw me and my best friend Archibald coming. It wasn't scream tag, like Grenway, Archibald's older brother said. My beginnings had more twists and turns than Tommy Harken's cat's tail after it was slammed in the screen door.

"It's hard to believe, I know, but here it is in black and white." Griggs waved her hand over the scrapbook. "Plain as the nose on your face, can't dispute that."

I wasn't disputing anything. For all I knew, everything Oswald Elliot drew was the gospel truth. It just made me feel a little naked showing my underbelly to all and sundry.

I slid off the chesterfield when I heard the screen door open and Nan step into the kitchen.

CHAPTER 4

I TWITCHED ALL the way home from Griggs' house. I didn't care about stepping on cracks or breaking mothers' backs. I didn't even take the time to look for the earthworms that might need saving. I always saved the earthworms, laid them in the grass where they could dry out before burrowing back down into the black earth. Touching their silky bodies, wondering if they soaked in some fancy dish soap. Once they were saved, I'd squat nearby to chase off any robins waiting to pick them off. I'd squat until my legs ached from the effort.

"What's wrong?" Nan asked. "We've passed three mud puddles, and you haven't stirred one."

The itch in the back of my throat slid up to the tip of my tongue, but I choked it back down. "Nothing's wrong."

"Well something's bothering you." Nan touched my forehead with the back of her hand. "No fever."

"Nope." The more Nan inquired, the more I felt out of sorts, just like Hester Prynne from *The Scarlet Letter*. Nan never told me normal kid stories. She said if her eyes didn't start bleeding from reading *Hop on Pop*, she'd pray for blindness.

Instead, she read what she called the classics; some I liked, some put me to sleep.

"You haven't done your Frankenstein walk either."

"Yeah, it's only fun in my pinchy church shoes." I couldn't tell Nan that Hester Prynne didn't have pinchy church shoes. A practical girl like her couldn't afford such luxuries.

Nan grabbed my shoulders and forced me front and centre; she bent down close so that her face was in mine. "What's got into you? You look like the cat that's swallowed the canary."

I wanted to tell her everything, about all the cartoon faces and Griggs' careful colouring of my should-have-been pa's rusty truck, the windswept nurses and Mayor Forde. The only thing that stopped me was the thought of Old Lady Griggs' skinless body, and how it would stick to her plastic-covered chesterfield. That and the thought of how Hester Prynne would be so disappointed. That woman could have her fingernails pulled out and she'd still keep her secret.

"I asked you a question, Celia, and I'm waiting for an answer." Nan's voice was losing its patience.

I squished my lips together, hoping to stop up what was bubbling inside of me, but it churned and churned until I couldn't control it any longer. "Old Lady Griggs —"

"Excuse me," Nan's voice was tight with a sharp edge.

"Mrs. Griggs," I corrected myself, "has a plastic-covered chesterfield." It was a relief saying it out loud. Like a weight had been lifted off. Now that Nan knew the truth she'd think twice about sharpening her knives.

"And what does that have to do with the price of rice in China?"

"Nothing. I just thought you should know, when I sit on it, the back of my legs stick. Can you imagine what would happen if I didn't have my skin on?"

Nan stood there looking at me for a long time. "My God child, I swear you grow stranger by the day."

"It was Old Lady Griggs that got me thinking about it."

Nan squeezed my shoulders one more time before letting me go. "I'm not sure the two of you are a good combination."

For the rest of the evening Nan didn't mention anything about cats and canaries. Not at dinner, or when she scrubbed behind my ears; not even when we said my bedtime prayer. But that didn't stop me from wanting to tell her about the big black scrapbook Griggs had hidden under her chesterfield. It sat on the end of my tongue, wanting to jump off every time I opened my mouth. And that night, when I closed my eyes, pencil-coloured faces stared back at me from my dreams.

In the morning Nan informed me that the next time she needed someone to mind me, she'd make other arrangements. She said she didn't want to wear out my welcome at Mrs. Griggs', as she was only a last resort.

"You're going to come to the Happy Valley Druggist with me," she said, brushing my hair. "Doesn't that sound like fun?"

"Not really. Griggs and me have a pot and pan band."

"Well band practice will have to wait," she said, putting in my last pigtail. She added blue ribbons to match my blue-checkered dress.

I could feel tears but blinked them away. Not going to Griggs' was like missing Christmas. How else was I going to find out about my should-have-beens? Nan wasn't going to tell me, and if I asked about them, she'd cotton on to what Griggs and me were up to and never let me see her again. "All right," I said, "but what am I going to do?"

"You'll oversee spiderwebs and dust bunnies," Nan said excitedly.

I rolled my eyes. "Dust bunnies aren't real."

"Real dust, fake bunnies, but they could be real, if you want them to be. A real Barnum and Bailey Circus."

Before spending my mornings with Griggs, having a spiderweb and dust bunny circus would have been appealing. Dust bunnies getting caught in sticky webs, only to be freed by the brave ringmaster? Now that's entertainment. But after the scrapbook, it seemed kind of boring.

"Can I charge money?" I asked.

"That depends on the act," Nan said, hurrying me out the door.

The mud puddles had dried up from the afternoon before, and I was disappointed that there were no earthworms to save. I avoided the cracks, but even that couldn't keep my attention. So, I did the only other thing I could do, I Frankenstein-walked all the way to the drugstore, and by the time I got there my draggy leg was so cramped I couldn't use it right.

"Walk properly," Nan said. "You're embarrassing me."

"I am walking properly," I said, swinging my crampy leg out to the side.

Nan smiled so tight I could hardly see the lipstick on her teeth. "I swear Celia, if you don't behave —"

"You'll skin me alive?"

"Something like that." Nan pushed open the door to the drugstore, and I followed her inside. I'd been there hundreds of times, but even so, every time I walked through the door, my jaw dropped in wonder. The one rule, the only rule, I had to follow in that place, was to keep my hands in my pockets. Luckily my blue checkered dress had two square pockets trimmed with lace. I wandered up and down the aisles, pretending to look for dust bunnies and spiderwebs but what I was really eyeing was the gumball machine. If I had a penny I would buy one of the big delicious gumballs; I didn't even care what colour it was.

It might have been my crampy leg, or the fact that I was

trying on sunglasses without using my hands, but whatever it was, when I rounded the gumball corner for the third time, I fell headfirst into the display. The machine broke and gumballs scattered everywhere, tripping anyone who didn't have the sense to look where they were going. When Nan was busy rounding up gumballs and sweeping up the glass, I pocketed three of the little devils.

Nan was in the middle of scooping and glaring at me when Mrs. Whitford, the druggist's wife, came rushing up the aisle oblivious to Nan crawling around on all fours. "Oh, Miss Canterberry, there you are. I'm in desperate need of your services."

Nan stood and ran her hands down her Happy Valley Druggist apron. "My services?"

"Yes, my hair appointment has been changed to," she tapped her watch, "ten minutes from now, and I need someone to mind my darlings." She looked back at the two little girls standing in the doorway that separated their living quarters from the drugstore. "They won't be any bother. If I don't go to the beauty salon, I won't make it to my afternoon meeting of The Ladies of the Perpetual Indigence Society. Everyone in our society gets their hair done. 'Tweezed, Cinched and Coiffed', that's our motto. Proper grooming is essential." She looked Nan up and down and sniffed.

Mrs. Whitford looked so pitiful I almost offered to do her hair myself.

Nan looked at the girls and then back to me. "I'd like to help you Mrs. Whitford, but I've got my hands full."

"Oh, don't worry about your little crippled girl," Mrs. Whitford said, fussing with the caved inside of her beehive hairdo. "I'm sure my girls and she will get on famously."

"It's not just that," Nan said. "Mr. Whitford has stepped out and left me in charge of the till."

"Please Miss Canterberry, we can make an exception this time, can't we?" She batted her glued-on lashes. "I would be ever so grateful." She batted once more as if Nan was supposed to be swayed by her charms like some common man, but Nan looked resigned to misery. Mrs. Whitford clapped her hands and headed for the door. "Don't be such a worry wart! What trouble can three little girls get into?"

When the door closed, Nan grunted. "The Ladies of the Perpetual Indigence Society, my Aunt Fanny. They don't know the meaning of the word. Not a single one of them! Confused indulgence with indigence most likely."

"A rookie mistake," I said with a shrug. The Dictionary Game had vastly expanded my vocabulary. Obviously, no one in the society had played that game.

"Exactly." Nan rubbed the back of her neck. "And to top it all off, as much as I despise each and every one of them, I don't have the heart to correct them. It would take a little bit of joy out of my life if they knew the true meaning." She took me by the hand and led me to the back of the store. "I just want you to play with the girls quietly. No roughhousing."

I nodded and looked at the two empty-headed blinkers in their matching pinafores. They could have been baby owls dropped purposely from the nest. "I will, Nan."

She bit at her nails and took a ragged breath. I don't think she'd have gone back to the till at all if it hadn't been for Mrs. Harkens, who was pounding the bell on the counter, asking for something to put on her cat's crooked tail to ease his misery and stop the yowling. The first slam it hadn't been so bad, but that morning Tommy had tried to straighten it out with a second one.

I sat cross-legged on the floor. "What would you like to do?" I asked, knowing full well I was company and the decision should be mine.

The sisters blinked twice but didn't say a word.

"Want to play a game?"

More blinking. This was going nowhere. I looked at the four-year-old. She was so peppered with freckles it was hard to find shapes in them. "Bet I can connect your cheek freckles with a felt pen and make a picture of a Lassie dog."

"Bet you can't."

I leaned closer. "Well maybe not a Lassie dog, but marzipan for sure. I could make a picture of that."

"Marzipan? What's marzipan?"

I looked at her as if I were in shock. "You don't know what marzipan is?"

She shook her head.

I didn't know what marzipan was either; Nan used all kinds of strange words with me and sometimes the meanings didn't stick. Hence, I made something up. "We talked about marzipan almost every day in my Grade One science class. Marzipan is what happens when you put two different things together." I clapped my hands. "Voila! Marzipan."

The sisters looked at each other before turning back to me. "Wow," they said in unison. It was as if I'd told them the moon wasn't made of cheese.

"You guys are dull as dishwater," I said, tweaking their noses. "Good thing you're cute as buttons."

My fingers twitched. I leaned over and touched the two-year-old's blond pigtail curls. If there ever was Rumpelstiltskin hair spun of fine gold, that was it. That curl bounced in my hand like a spring. I touched my own pigtails. They stood straight up like strange little gophers waiting to be run over by a car.

"She has alabaster skin," said the four-year-old.

"*Alabaster* skin," I said, kind of impressed. "Sounds like something hard." I flicked her head with my finger. "I bet I could bounce my pocket change, if I had any, off of her cranium."

The four-year-old shook her head. "My mother wouldn't like that."

"Figures." My fingers started to twitch again and found the gumballs in my pocket. "Want to see a trick?" The girls nodded. I popped the blue ball in my mouth and chewed until the ball turned into a wad, then I spat it out and flattened it in the palm of my hand, then popped it back into my mouth and tried to blow a bubble. I blew so hard it flew out of my mouth and into one of the blond loops. When I tried to snatch it out, the littlest owl started to scream.

"Hold on, alabaster girl," I said. "If your mother finds out I was chewing gum with my mouth open, we'll both be in trouble. Me for chewing and you for standing too close." The more I pried, the more she wiggled and fussed. I stepped back to examine her; she appeared a bit lopsided with one pigtail dangling free while the other was a lump tucked close to the hair ribbon that bound it. "Oh, dear. Your mother is not going to like this." I paused and looked around. "Where're the scissors?"

I'd only stapled hair, I wasn't very good at cutting it, and I cut a little too close to her alabaster scalp. So, I did the only thing a reasonable person would do. I coloured in the bare patches with a Jiffy marker and gave the girls my two remaining gumballs to stop them from crying.

After that, whenever Nan worked a shift at the Happy Valley Druggist, Griggs and me were inseparable.

CHAPTER 5

THE NEXT TIME I showed up at Old Lady Griggs' house she was colouring to beat the band. "I heard what happened at the Happy Valley Druggist," she said, without even raising her head. "It's all right here."

I looked over her shoulder, examining each box in the cartoon panel spread out on her kitchen table. There they were, the owl children in their matching pinafores, the younger all dishevelled, like she'd escaped from prison by digging herself out with a spoon; Mrs. Whit-ford pulling hysterically at her new beehive hairdo with her manicured fingers; Nan all forlorn in her drugstore apron, looking like things couldn't get much worse.

"Yup, that's how it happened," I said. "But I didn't know the newspaper was still covering my shenanigans."

"Of course they are. But you could have told me you were going to be putting on a performance! But no, don't tell Mrs. Griggs, the only one willing to risk life and limb just to show you your dismal beginnings. I wish I'd been there." Her lips curled as she snapped a pencil crayon in half. "It makes me cross just thinking about it."

Griggs had a way of appreciating things that Nan took for granted. My performance at the druggist hadn't raised even a glimmer of pride in Nan's eye, yet Griggs sat fuming over my comic strip, her pencil crayons bringing out possibilities that even my little mind hadn't envisioned. I had to admire her for it.

"Nan told me I should have kept my hands to myself."

"Maybe you should have." Griggs got up and walked over to the kitchen counter to grab the scotch tape. There she retaped the two jagged ends of the pencil crayon together. "But who in their right mind *wouldn't* have taken advantage of such a plum opportunity?"

"That's what I thought," I said, relaxing a little.

"That being said, Molly was lucky she wasn't fired on the spot."

"That would have been something to see, Nan getting fired. I bet she'd swell up like a puffer fish."

"Oswald would have had a field day drawing that. Folks would probably find it more entertaining than our Pin the Tail on the Donkey games."

"With Job?" I asked.

"No," Griggs snapped. "What's your obsession with that man?"

I sighed. "Just trying to place him, that's all." I looked back down at the strip. Griggs had picked up her India ink pen and was adding flourishes to Mrs. Whitford's hair; it looked like a mini tornado, all kinds of sticks and terrified little baby animals peeking out between the swirls, their tiny cheeks puffed out as if they were about to explode.

"I don't remember her hair looking like that."

"Well I can't say, I wasn't there. But I'm sure that's how it felt." Griggs lifted the pen from the page and tilted her head this way and that before adding a few more swirls. "Every time that woman enters a room it's like she's the Queen of Sheba, wants the rest of us to bow and scrape."

"I think she just wanted Nan to sweep up the locks," I said, remembering the broom that flew across the room, beaning Mr. Whitford in the head. Griggs kept adding to Mrs. Whitford's woebegone wailing. Her perfectly manicured hands were morphing into trotters, still bright pink at the tips. The empty box of Kleenex she'd held so daintily in the drugstore, was now, in the comic strip, being crushed in her swollen piggy hands. Used tissues piled up around her piggy feet, threatening to cover her least favourite owl child. To top it all off, her glued-on eyelashes were pulling up at the edges.

As Old Lady Griggs' pen scratched new lines and shaded new edges, Oswald Elliot's old shapes vanished beneath her strokes. I hadn't noticed her changes when she'd first shown me the drawings — I think she was a stay-between-the-lines colouring person then — but now, as I watched her fingers gather steam, they flitted from one box to another, changing things that Oswald Elliot would have been tarred and feathered for publishing. That is if he dared to think them up in the first place. Griggs even added a few boxes of her own.

In one box Mrs. Whitford was all buggy-eyed, not seeming to care about the tiny creatures clinging to her tornado beehive hairdo. And in the next she was striking at them with her trotters. Griggs said a little Bedlam never hurt anyone. As for Mr. Whitford, Griggs changed his white lab coat into some kind of evil overlord cape. The villainy suited him, especially the way he eyed the youngest of his owl children, particularly the black spot on the side of her head. It was just visible over top the pile of tissues she wallowed in. He didn't step closer and tenderly lift her from the debris, as might be expected from a loving father. Instead he leaned down and rubbed the spot with as much glee as a medieval scientist who's just discovered alchemy. He didn't even seem to see her. His twitchy fingers rubbed that Jiffy permanent marker spot so much it was a wonder there was still skin left on it.

Griggs paused and looked at me. "All these years I've lived in Happy Valley and I have yet to make an appearance in your strip. I've been mentioned, but never drawn. Even though I've gone uninvited to your christening, birthday parties, and kindergarten graduation — and still Oswald hasn't included me. Why do you think that is?"

"I didn't go to kindergarten," I said, tapping her on the shoulder.

Griggs' voice hardened. "Hence the waste of time attending it. All that Whitford woman had to do was flounce off to the beauty parlour. If I'd known that's all it took," her voice trailed off and she looked bewildered. Her eyes widened, the lazy one a little slower than the ambitious one, as if it was wary of outdoing its better. "But no matter where I go or what I do, I've either come too late, or left too early and missed the bizarre stuff altogether. I'm almost ready to throw in the towel." She held up an orangey-yellow pencil. "I've even picked out my hair colour."

"That's pretty." I wanted to tell her that one day she'd make it into the strip. That there was no shame in being an afterthought; public humiliation was just around the corner if she played her cards right.

Griggs rubbed the back of her husband's nylon hand. "If I were to be front and centre in your comic strip panel, Mr. Griggs would be so proud. I wouldn't hear the end of it for a month of Sundays. As it is, I'm at my wits end."

I stood there waiting for Griggs to finish her work of art. She didn't seem to be in any particular hurry and I assumed she was colouring away her disappointment. To encourage her I clicked my tongue against the roof of my mouth, like a countdown clock. Griggs paused, tapped her crayon and raised her gaze to me. There was no tenderness in it. "Do you think that nonsense would work on Leonardo da Vinci? Michelangelo? Charles Dickens? Were they rushed to complete their masterpieces?"

"No."

"That's right. And your clucking won't work on me either." She closed her eyes and took a slow deep breath, letting it escape in puffs from between her tightly pursed lips. "And before you point out that Charles Dickens wasn't an artist, let me tell you something, smarty pants, he painted in words." With one last stroke, Griggs finished her colouring, leaned back and examined the page. A look of exultation crossed her face. "There," she said, "it is finished."

Griggs kissed her husband on his cotton-stuffed cheek before high-stepping it over the pots and pans into the living room, freshly coloured comic strip in one hand, Elmer's glue in the other. She opened the black scrapbook and pasted her new addition in the next empty spot. It wasn't one of her best renderings — too much emotion, not enough depth — but who was I to judge?

"You know," Griggs said, as I scooched up beside her. "Your should-have-been ma left as soon as that cord was cut. Nurses said she couldn't get out of there fast enough. Never even asked if you were a boy or girl. Didn't even wait to be properly cleaned up."

I didn't know what to say. No one had ever talked to me about babies before, so it was hard for me to tell if my should-have-been was just like every other mother. But with Griggs frowning and shaking her head, I figured she probably wasn't. "What did my Nan say?"

"Your Nan? She didn't know anything more about your mother than I did. Audrey was wiggly, always had been. She's been disappearing as soon as she was old enough to crawl out her bedroom window and shimmy down the drain pipe. And as soon as it was legal to drop out of school, she took to the road. That girl went from county to county living in old sheds, abandoned barns, or in that old pickup truck. On any given day your Nan couldn't say where the girl was or who she was with. Audrey was a bouncer and nothing could be done about it. I think that's the only reason she came to the hospital. You can't bounce with a baby."

Audrey. I let the name wander around in my head a little before balancing it on the tip of my tongue. It was a hard name to say without half closing my eyes and imagining myself holding a long skinny cigarette. "Oh," I said. I wanted to ask if Nan liked bouncing. If she didn't want a baby any more than my should-have-been did. If she didn't, where was that going to leave me? Standing alone on the side of the road while Nan thumbed her way across the prairies? I think the only thing that was stopping her were her shoes. She always said if she had extra money she'd buy herself a good pair of shoes. Shoes that would take her away from me. Griggs must have known what I was thinking cause she started explaining how Nan was different, always had been.

"Your Nan," she said. "She's a firebrand that one. Doesn't matter what happens to her, she thrusts her shoulders back and holds her head high. Never shirks her responsibilities. Did everything she could to keep your mother on the straight and narrow. More than anyone could expect of her," Griggs smiled and ruffled my hair.

I didn't like the idea of being one of Nan's responsibilities. I wanted to be more than that. I wanted to be her one best thing.

Griggs changed the subject. "When she was younger, we used her rump for Pin the Tail on the Donkey. Not your should-have-been, your Nan. She was such a good sport. Come to think of it, it might have done your should-have-been some good to get jabbed in the arse once in a while."

"That wasn't very nice. No wonder Job wouldn't play."

Griggs bristled. "We were kids. Besides, your Nan didn't seem to mind. She didn't wear a blindfold and got to kick like a mule at anyone making their approach; we always ended up with more bruises than she got pin pricks. Those were fine times. But never mind that now. I was telling you about your unusual birthing." She flipped to a different page in the scrapbook. "Here it is." She cleared her throat, and made her singsong voice come out. *Nurse Timmer grips the sides of the door frame, the length of her fingers white with the effort.* "You're not leaving here without your spawn," *she commands. But the should-have-been ma does not heed. Her vile face reddens and her nostrils flare as she charges the God-fearing nurse, knocking the innocent lamb to the floor.*

"Oh," Nurse Timmer whimpers, as Doc Marley rushes to her aid. "I'm so distraught, so very distraught." She presses the back of her pale hand to her forehead.

Looking towards the exit, where the should-have-been ma is fleeing, Doc Marley shakes his fist and shouts a curse to the particleboard ceiling. "Damn you, damn you to hell."

Nurse Timmer buries her face in the doctor's shoulder and weeps at the indignity of it all.

Old Lady Griggs looked up from the book and sighed. "Isn't that romantic?"

I made a face. "Doc Marley looks old enough to be Nurse Timmer's grandpa."

"He is." Griggs kissed the tips of her fingers and placed them on the doctor's cartoon face. "But that's how some women like it, an older, richer man, ready and willing to rescue them."

As far as I was concerned Nurse Timmer didn't need rescuing. She needed to get up off the floor and wallop my should-have-been ma, and leave Doc Marley hobbling behind with his cane. But that's not how Griggs saw it. She fussed and mooned over that cartoon picture as if it were the real thing. I was just about to go into the kitchen and tell her husband she was acting foolish when she came to her senses.

"Everyone expected that your should-have-been would leave without you. No one thought any less of her for it, it was almost impossible to do that. Your Nan said even as a girl she'd never been much for nurturing; just as soon snap the heads off her dolls as play with them. A contortionist if ever there was one, twisting herself into the most peculiar situations to escape responsibility and repercussions. But when you came along, well that was one predicament that she couldn't wiggle free of, so she became the vanishing girl instead." Griggs licked a finger. "I suppose it's for the best. Who wants no-account drifters for parents?"

I wanted to put up my hand. It wasn't that I didn't want Nan to be my real ma, my everyday ma, but it might be fun to have a sometimes ma and pa who had adventures and sometimes bounced, who could take me to the beach or throw a ball. But to say it out loud would sound ungrateful, like I didn't heed Griggs' warning about Job, the guy who hated singalongs and Pin the Tail on the Donkey, but who had a lot of patience. All I could do was sit there and let the back of my sweaty legs glue themselves to the plastic-covered chesterfield.

The next headline read, *What Child is This?* Griggs had added devil horns to some of the letters.

"Never mind those," she said, seeing my concern. "They're for comic relief."

"I don't feel relieved," I said. I'd been hoping she used her extras for the Whitfords and the PIS Ladies, but that she kept her pencils to herself when it came to me and Nan.

She shifted and the plastic made crinkly sounds under her bony posterior, as if she couldn't find the sweet spot. "Oh, looky here, there's your Nan."

I looked to where Griggs indicated, and sure as shooting, there was Nan. She looked more frazzled than usual, her hair all discombobulated. I wouldn't be surprised if her paisley dress was tucked into the back of her panties; it was hard to tell, the way Oswald drew her. Old Lady Griggs started reading a few panels back before Nan entered the picture.

Nurse Timmer, delivered from her delirium, staggers towards the phone, the ever-faithful Doc Marley by her side. "Just one foot in front of the other," he soothes.

"I don't know if I can do it," Nurse Timmer swoons.

"You have to, goddamnit. You have to."

Jutting out her chin, Nurse Timmer gathers whatever fortitude she has remaining and picks up the receiver to dial the number. The phone rings for what feels like an eternity as the eminent Doc Marley props her up and fans her with a manila folder.

Meanwhile, Molly Canterberry toils in her garden, ignoring the ringing phone, all but turning her back on her societal obligations — a fact that doesn't go unnoticed by her more godly neighbours and The Ladies of the Perpetual Indigence Society.

"For heaven's sake, can't a person get a second's peace?" She looks back towards the house. The phone continues ringing, so she apologizes to the potato plant she was relieving of bugs. "We will continue this conversation later," she says to the plant. "There seems to be a more pressing matter to attend to."

I folded my arms in protest, nudging Griggs repeatedly with an elbow.

"What is it now?"

"I know that part isn't true."

"How would you know? You weren't there."

I gave a knowing shrug.

Griggs scanned the page, looking for something she'd overlooked.

"Look harder," I encouraged.

"At what?" Griggs' voice had lost all its singsonginess.

"The piece with Nan in the garden."

"The whole thing is about your Nan in the garden."

"Look at her face, the part where you didn't add anything."

"I've never added anything to her visage. It speaks for itself." Griggs grew indignant, and leaned closer. "What's wrong with it?"

"Everything." I waited. Griggs wasn't any better at this game than she was at the dictionary one. She didn't even have the imagination to make something up. I was afraid she was going to wear out the paper with all her beady-eye scanning. "Her teeth," I blurted.

"They look perfectly fine to me." Griggs adjusted her glasses and leaned so close there was hardly any room between her and the scrapbook. "There's nothing caught between them and she's wearing both the tops and bottoms."

"That's just it, she never wears her teeth when she's gardening. She thinks it's best not to let the plants know her true intentions."

"Did she tell you that? It's the most ridiculous thing I've ever heard, and your Nan is the least ridiculous person I know."

"She didn't have to tell me. What other reason could there be?" I rolled my eyes as if I would expire from exasperation. "Occam's razor."

Griggs nodded but I knew she didn't know what an Occam's razor was, any more than I did. But I'd heard Nan use those words enough times that I could put them in a sentence without sounding like a complete idiot. Drove my Grade One teacher, Miss Dobbs, crazy. She even told Nan, at a parent teacher interview, that I wasn't allowed to use it for all my test answers. That I was old enough to use the expected response. After that I used it only occasionally, to watch Miss Dobbs redden when she was marking, and keep her circulation regular.

Old Lady Griggs let the matter drop, even though I knew there were unsaid words on her tongue, and went back to reading.

Brushing her hands off on the front of her apron, Miss Canterberry trudges towards the house. The phone is still ringing when she enters the kitchen. It almost vibrates off the wall with its own importance. "Hello," *she says, irritated by the interruption.*

"Miss Canterberry?"

"Yes."

"Oh, thank God." *There is a pause.* "We thought you were dead."

"Who is this?"

"Nurse Timmer from the Happy Valley Hospital. We're calling to inform you that a package has been delivered and you need to pick it up."

Miss Canterberry sinks onto the high stool she keeps beneath her wall phone. "What kind of package?"

Nurse Timmer covers the mouthpiece with the palm of her hand and confers with Doc Marley.

"Doc Marley said you have to come see for yourself."

"Well can't it keep?" *Miss Canterberry looks out her kitchen window towards her neglected garden.* "Doc Marley knows I've been busy looking in on Mrs. Griggs and this is the first moment I've had to myself."

"No ma'am, it can't wait. Doc Marley says this package is far more important than Mrs. Griggs' bursitis. We'll send a car to pick you up directly."

"What if I don't want to be picked up directly?"

There is no answer; the line is already dead.

At the bottom of the page, instead of turning it, as I'd

expected, Griggs paused and began humming. She flicked her fingers as if she were trying to conduct music. The kind they have at a motion picture show, her body wiggling and waggling. I couldn't pick out the tune and soon lost patience. "What happens next?" I leaned across Griggs and tried to turn the page myself.

"Hand's off." Griggs blocked my attempt as she continued her flicking. "We're almost there." Her arms were now above her head, the flicking ended with a lightning clap of her hands. "The crescendo," she said, before letting out a deep breath and stilling. "Now the pregnant pause."

"Can we get back to your colouring?" I asked.

Griggs huffed as her wonky eyes came back into focus. "We never left." She cracked her knuckles and turned the page. "There is much more to what I do than breathe life into Oswald Elliot's miserable depictions, which I find both flat and uninspired." Her lazy eye bulged with purpose. Its independence was rousing. "And if you want me to continue reading you need to sit still and be patient while I chase the muse."

I nodded and neatly folded my hands in my lap, just the way I had seen a freckle-faced pigtail girl pose in the Sears catalogue; the one with the staple through her cheek, to help hold her to the spot.

Griggs didn't seem to care about my predicament, she was too busy taking deep breaths and smacking her lips. But no matter how hard she beckoned, that muse-guy wouldn't slow down or come out of hiding. I blinked hard, trying to summon a tear of solidarity, considering how frustrated she must be getting, but I was a little dehydrated. The more I tried, the more my lids stuck to my eyeballs. What if my eyeballs dried out and popped right out of my head? I'd never be able to see my cartoon should-have-beens again, and the kids at school might want to use my hollowed-out eye sockets to store their erasers. Occam's razor.

In time, Griggs gave up on muse-chasing and picked up where she'd left off. "After the phone call from Nurse Timmer, one of Bill McNealy's boys came for your Nan," she explained.

"Here it is." *The car pulls into Molly Canterberry's drive about the same time she hangs up the receiver. She has just enough time to put on a sweater and grab her handbag.* "Miss Canterberry," *the driver says, as he opens the door and bows slightly at the waist,* "your chariot awaits."

"What's all the fuss about?" *she asks, slipping into the backseat of the car.* "Honestly I've lived in Happy Valley all my life and this is the first time anyone has sent a car to fetch me."

"Your guess is good as mine," *the driver says, cranking down his window.*

"Aren't you the McNealy boy, the one who got his head stuck in the railing at the Happy Valley Druggist?"

"Could be."

"Do you think your father would approve of you forcing an old woman into a hot car in the middle of the day, just because Doc Marley tells you to? It's ludicrous."

"I didn't force you, ma'am."

"It feels that way to me." *Miss Canterberry unbuttons her sweater and fans herself with her hand.* "It's hot as Hades in here."

"Yes, ma'am."

"I'd roll down my window, but it will wreak havoc on my hair." *She glimpses Bill Jr. rolling his eyes in the rear-view mirror.* "I saw that," *she snaps.* "Young people these days, no respect for their elders. Think you can ridicule me, thinking I'm too daft to notice? I'll talk to your father, that's what I'll do."

The car speeds up, forcing Miss Canterberry to cease her

complaining and concentrate on bracing herself to keep from toppling over.

She arrives at the Happy Valley Hospital dishevelled and unnerved.

Nurse Timmer shelters under the overhang at the building's main door, as if she were avoiding the onset of foul weather. She waves the newcomer in. "Hurry," *she says, sticking her head from under the covering.* "They might come back."

"Who?"

"You'll see," *the nurse says, leading the other inside.* "But I warn you, it might take you a while to get over the shock."

"What shock?"

"Of the baby."

"Whose baby?"

Nurse Timmer turns. "Don't you know?"

Miss Canterberry runs her hands through her tousled locks. "How am I supposed to know anything when you talk in riddles?"

"Don't shout at her!" *Doc Marley comes lumbering down the hallway towards the pair, the sound of his cane punctuating his displeasure.* "She's been through enough, poor lamb." *His eyes narrow as he turns towards Molly Canterberry.* "As I expected, you're behaving just like your daughter."

"My daughter?" *Molly Canterberry stiffens.*

"Yes, your daughter. The one who marched in here earlier today, screeching and making demands like she owned the place. That girl hasn't changed a bit, just as unthinking and inhuman as ever. Never seen anything like it. And need I remind the pair of you this is a hospital, not some common bawdy house?"

Miss Canterberry reddens. "You needn't remind me of anything and why you've dragged me all the way down here to tell me so, is beyond me. A complete waste of my time." She steps to the shrivelled physician. "And need I remind you…"

Doc Marley puts up his hand. "That won't be necessary."

"I should hope not." Miss Canterberry turns to leave.

"Not so fast." The good doctor catches her arm with the hook of his cane. "You're not escaping without that." His lip curls as his gaze fixes on a bundle lying in a rickety wicker basinet.

Miss Canterberry hesitates before turning to the mewling pile. "What do we have here?"

"Your grandbaby," Doc Marley said. "The first and hopefully the last."

"Mine?" She steps closer and lifts a corner of the receiving blanket to peer down at the tiny face.

"It doesn't spit acid," Doc Marley says, by way of encouragement.

"It's not that. I didn't even know my girl was pregnant."

"That's the way it is with some families, they breed like feral cats, always in heat, roaming to whoever will have them, and then shunning the consequences."

Miss Canterberry doesn't respond to the doctor, but stands there, examining the foundling while he shakes with disapproval. "See this," he bellows, grabbing hold of Nurse Timmer by the wrist and jerking her forward. "If you have any doubts, cast your eyes here." He indicates the scratches and welts rising on the nurse's china-bone arms. "Isn't this proof enough? Who else but your daughter could have done such a thing, I ask you that?"

Miss Canterberry gives no answer.

Nurse Timmer withdraws as he trots in Nurse Todd, still in a vegetated state. "And if you still had any doubts take a gander at her. If the drooling isn't a dead giveaway, the blank stare certainly is." His face trembles with indignation. "To prevent further hullabaloo, it would be greatly appreciated if you'd do whatever needs to be done to rectify the matter. The ladies here would prefer if that girl of yours has no reason to return."

"And how in God's name am I going to prevent that?"

Doc Marley leans forward. "Take that thing," he says, showing a flash of teeth, before remembering his position, his oath. He clears his throat and corrects himself, softening his tone. "The child, take it home."

Miss Canterberry runs a finger down the infant's cheek. "She's hardly dried off."

"She's dry enough, besides, she's strong and healthy."

Biting her lip, the new grandmother refuses the smock Nurse Timmer holds up between two fingers. Instead she rummages around in her handbag until she pulls out an old tea towel. The one she'd used to wrap the previous week's church potluck casserole. "I don't need your charity," she says, her eyes brimming. "I don't need anyone's charity."

Doc Marley sucks the inside of his cheek. "The mayor will be relieved. The last thing this town needs is more charity cases."

CHAPTER 6

GRIGGS DABBED her forehead with a wrinkled hanky. She said, to her chagrin, she was starting to glisten. "That's what happens to us theatre people. We give so much, our essence oozes out."

"Like pus?" I pointed to the full-grown droplets of perspiration peppering her brow.

"No, not like pus." Griggs' face pinched together. "Sometimes you say the most god-awful things. Between you and your Nan it's a wonder that I can function at all. The way that woman looks at me, it's only a matter of time before the chickens come home to roost."

"Don't worry," I told her. "You locked the door. No one is getting in."

"Your Nan knows that lock doesn't work. I was making a statement."

At her insistence I rent myself free from the plastic-covered chesterfield and trotted over to the living room window. Griggs was right, she had reason to glisten. Through the dusty lace curtains I could see Nan stomping down the street. In a flash,

Griggs had stowed the scrapbook, navigated her way around the pots and pans, and was at my side.

"If you hadn't spent so much time flicking your fingers," I said bitterly, "We'd be half way through the scrapbook right now."

"It's not about how far you go, but how deep. There's no getting around it, Celia Canterberry," she said, not taking her eyes off Nan. "I feel sorry for you. To be so blind to the subtleties of an artistic endeavour such as muse-chasing, is akin to being deaf to the midnight callings of a nightshade plant."

I wanted to tell her plants don't call, not even at midnight, but Nan was advancing on Griggs's house, and it wouldn't be long until she burst through the door to give her usual greeting to Mr. Griggs. It would be unseemly to be arguing with his Mrs. about talking plants and a scrapbook that wasn't supposed to exist.

"She wasn't wearing that when she left this morning," I said, turning my attention back to Nan. "She looks fit to be tied."

"That she does," Griggs tutted. "I don't know what possessed her to put that on. The druggist must have been handing out samples."

Nan was in a fluorescent pink polyester jumpsuit. Culottes. Just like Cher when she was singing *I got you Babe*. If Cher were dirt poor and had been stung by a million bees. "She's missing the headband," I said.

"I don't think it would help."

When Nan met us at the front door, Griggs spoke to her through the screen, a little unsure of Nan's state of mind. "Molly?"

"Dorigen." Nan's lips were tight, daring us to question her about her outfit. "Hope she wasn't too much trouble."

"No more than usual." Griggs opened the screen door just enough for me to squeeze through.

I watched Nan's face the whole time I made my escape. I wasn't sure what to make of it. Her cheek muscles jumped, her lips pursed, and her eyebrows were pinned together. I'd never seen her in such a state. We'd hardly gone ten steps down the walk when Old Lady Griggs called after us, "Just because you can wiggle into something doesn't mean you should wear it."

Nan turned on her heel. "You think I wiggled into this on purpose? That I would willingly, publicly humiliate myself? If you do, you're mistaken. She gestured to her attire. "This is Enid Whitford's idea of a work uniform. When I arrived this morning, she was waiting for me by the door with this atrocity draped over an arm. 'Miss Canterberry,' she said, sweet as pie, 'this showed up this morning.' As if I was daft enough to believe she wasn't behind the conspiracy. 'Oh,' I said, fingering the fabric. 'I'm sure you'll look lovely in it when you attend your next Ladies of the Perpetual Indigence Society meeting.' The bat snickered, 'Not me, you silly goose. This is for you. You'll look much more elegant when you're stocking the shelves. Try it on, you'll see.'

"After a standoff, I complied, if only to show the prude that her tastes were abysmal and, as she could plainly see, it was advisable that I change back into my former attire. When I went to retrieve my clothing, there was nothing to retrieve. 'Oh my.' Mrs. Whitford's eyes widened in mock surprise. 'Must have been thrown into the incinerator with the rest of the trash. I guess you have no choice now.' Hence my ongoing public humiliation." Nan balled her hands into fists. "If I didn't need the money I'd have quit on the spot."

Griggs opened the screen door and ventured on to the step. "On second thought, it's really not that bad, Molly. In the right light, and if you shed a few pounds, it could be rather fetching."

Nan's shoulders slumped. "The only upshot is I won't have

to wear it again. Mr. Whitford had a fit. 'If we're not selling it, we're not flaunting it,' he said."

"That's a relief," Griggs said. "Can't see myself taking the druggist seriously with a painted hussy on staff. No offence."

Nan didn't respond to Griggs's comment. Instead she thanked her once more for taking care of me and turned for home.

"What layer was it today?" I asked, as soon as we were out of earshot.

"The fifth," she said, plucking hot pink fabric from her butt crack.

"You hate that layer."

"I hate all the layers."

Since going to work for the Happy Valley Druggist, Nan had compared each day to a level in Dante's Inferno. The fifth was a typical day, as Mrs. Whitford wavered between being wrathful and sullen. Apparently, she hadn't gotten over her little owl baby's hair debacle, the tale of the lopped-sided pigtails. Mr. Whitford was no help, constantly calling the poor child to the front counter, making her expose her scalp—as if he was searching for head lice—to grown men standing around gaping as if it were one of the Seven Wonders of the World. "Look at that," Farmer Hempel had said, moving his toothpick from one side of his mouth to the other. "How long has that spot been there?"

"At least a month." Mr. Whitford lied, knowing full well that it hadn't been a fortnight. As he rubbed the spot, his owl daughter, the empty-headed little thing, just stood there, tilting her head this way and that, proud to please a man who'd hardly had the time of day for her before the marker incident. After a time, Mr. Whitford raised his hand and showed the other his thumb. "See? Clean as a whistle. Doesn't come off no matter how hard I rub it. That's the staying power of a permanent Jiffy marker."

Nan stiffened beside me. "He's the only man I know who'd use his own daughter as a marketing gimmick. And to tell you the truth, I think the fool's spent most of last evening recolouring the spot, darkening it up in hopes it will never fade." Nan quickened her pace as she went up the steps to her house. "And there in the background stands his wife. Whimpering and pulling tissue after tissue from her Kleenex box, utterly useless. The woman plants herself in that doorway to her residence, black mascara staining her cheeks, sniffing and carrying on like it's the end of the world. But not once does she try to stop him from his ludicrous promotions; hoping instead that selling one thing might lead to the sale of something else. Maybe they can get another shiny new car. Imagine that, profiting on another's misfortune? Misfortune that little owl girl doesn't even know she has yet."

Nan started supper and I stood there, glued to her elbow, while she peeled potatoes. "The thought of that woman riding around in a shiny new convertible, pink foam cocooning her beehive hair, is enough to do me in." Paring knife in hand Nan turned to me. "I'm sorry Celia, I shouldn't be telling you these things. Children should be left to be children, but sometimes this town makes that impossible."

I nodded. "That's what Old Lady Griggs thinks."

A potato plopped into the pot of water. "She told you that?"

"Not exactly. Occam's razor."

'Uh," Nan raised an eyebrow. "The law of parsimony."

Excitement almost overtook me. I could hardly think. We were playing the Dictionary Game and we hadn't even eaten supper! The only trouble was that I wasn't really sure what Occam's razor was, let alone the law of parsimony, but I was pretty sure I could make an educated guess. I took a potato peel and curled it around my wrist, just to buy time. "Indubitably?" I said after a long pause.

Nan turned on the burner and set the pot down. "Oh, sweet pea, close but no cigar." She leaned over and kissed me on the tip of my nose. I grunted and trudged off to fetch the dictionary.

CHAPTER 7

IN THE MORNING, Nan sent me out to the garden to pluck potato bugs and put them in a jar. I didn't mind the plucking, but I hated the sounds of the little fellas plinking against the glass as I dropped them into their captivity. It was when I was busy squatting and plinking that I spied Sneaky Walker and his mangy cat.

It wasn't the first time I'd spied Sneaky Walker, or Mr. Douglas as Nan insisted I call him. He lived two doors down from Nan, right beside Old Lady Griggs; Griggs sometimes caught him smelling her sheets on the line. I think he was as shocked as the rest of us that Griggs had sheets and didn't sleep in a coffin alongside Mr. Griggs, or hang by her heels in the cellar like a bat.

I spied Sneaky Walker nearly every day because he lived so close to Nan. He gave me the creeps. He was the reason I Frankenstein-walked; if he thought I was already dead or a mutant, he was less likely to kill me in my sleep. The last time he came over he was stark naked. Old Lady Griggs said Mr. Douglas used to be sweet on Nan, but if that was sweet, he had a funny way of showing it. He was all wrinkly, covered with bunches of hair and age spots. Nan was as surprised as me to see him there on the doorstep, wringing his hands like he'd forgotten how to knock. "Celia," Nan said in a strange voice, "go hide."

I nodded, hardly allowing myself to blink, but stayed where I was, taking in the whole of him.

"Celia." Nan's voice was sharper this time; she was in no mood for a negotiation.

I started backing up without turning around and slipped under the Christmas cactus that lived beneath the living room window. "I'll hide in plain sight," I called. "Just like a red-blooded spy, ready to jump out if needed."

"You do that," Nan said, but I don't think she was really listening. She'd stepped between the cactus and open door, blocking the best part of my view.

"Walter," I heard her say from my hideout. "It's nice to see you."

"But not all of him," I interjected loudly. "You need to tell him that."

Nan's head bobbed almost imperceptibly; this time she heard me, we were a team. I readjusted my position, my springy-legs had already begun to cramp under the three-legged stand. The problem was springing without snapping off any of the leaves, Nan would get cross at me for that. She treasured that plant and stand, as they had been a wedding gift to her grandmother. It wasn't my best hiding spot, but I wanted to be within earshot, in case things went sideways.

Sneaky Walker and Nan talked on the doorstep for quite some time. She asked him how his day was, and he asked her if she was enjoying the fine weather. He leaned on the door frame and said it reminded him of the days when they used to go walking together. Nan said that was a long time ago and they were different people back then. She lowered her voice and leaned in to him, making it hard for me to hear what she was saying. But from what I heard Nan never mention his clothes, as if standing there in his all-together were as common as rice pudding. She handed him a quilt and said he should wrap himself in it, so he didn't catch cold. He took it and thanked her.

When he was gone I asked Nan about him, but she didn't say much. We had just finished our supper and she'd handed me a dishtowel and told me to dry. Standing on my tiptoes I blew at the bubbles as water filled the kitchen sink. "Nan," I said, "can I ask you a question?"

"That depends on what the question is."

I blew at some more bubbles. "It's about Sneaky Walker."

Her jaw went tight, and her hands stilled in the dishwater. "What about him?"

"Arms and legs I've seen before." I paused trying to think of the right words, and sweat began to bead on my forehead. "Neck, head, ears, I've known what those things were as far back as I can remember. But there's one thing that's been puzzling me." I dipped my fingers in the dishwater. "What was that hangy down part?"

"Oh, that," Nan sighed as she handed me a plate. "That's his dangling participle."

"What's it for?"

"God only knows."

It seemed like a reasonable answer and I didn't question Nan further. But now that Sneaky Walker and Tiberius, his mangy cat, were back, I had more questions. Sneaky Walker et al. were on the other side of Nan's caraganas hedge hunting for something in the bushes. Whatever they were doing seemed far more interesting than plucking potato bugs. I set down my jar and went over to investigate.

"Mr. Douglas," I said, using his everyday name in case Nan was listening through the kitchen window, "don't you have your own caraganas to poke around in?"

Sneaky Walker grunted in my direction, and without looking up continued his poking. His cat, Tiberius, twitched his tail and walked figure eights around his master's legs. With every pass that mangy beast hissed and showed his teeth.

"Nan doesn't like anyone poking around in her things," I said, stepping a bit closer to see what the fuss was about, mindful of Tiberius.

With the end of a stick, Sneaky Walker jabbed at something that squealed and bolted from the greenery. It was the biggest, juiciest, rat I'd ever seen. I would have jumped out of my boots if I were wearing any. The mangy cat pounced on it before it got past the end of the hedge. The rat twitched as the cat crunched its skull in his jaws and carried it back to Sneaky Walker. He grabbed the rat by the tail and conked it on the head with his stick.

"Hmm, that must be your supper," I said in a voice with a gag in it. That's when an itchy feeling crawled down my spine. Nan was behind me, I could sense her. She grabbed me by the ear so hard that I was sure she was going to rip it right off my head and give it to Tiberius for dessert.

"Thank you, Mr. Douglas," she said, giving me a violent shake. "This morning when I saw that vermin lurking around the back shed, I knew you were the man for the job."

Sneaky Walker, holding the dead rat by the tail, nodded and turned back to his own yard. His mangy cat followed, swiping his mangy cat claws at the dead rat's bobbing head. It wasn't until Sneaky Walker was behind his own caragana hedge that Nan let me go. I rubbed my ear, while trying to push it closer to my head. With all her yanking it must have stood out a mile.

Nan thrust the potato-bug jar into my belly and pointed to the garden. I trudged all the way there just in case she was watching, so she'd think I felt shame and was in no need of further punishment.

I plucked more potato bugs than anyone else in the history of the world, and never complained once. My shirt was clinging to my sweaty back, and my throat was so dry I was sure it would stick shut. That made my breathing all tight and ragged. I was lucky to survive the morning.

At lunch time I was allowed to show the bug jar to Nan. I named most of the bugs and even though they begged me not to, I committed their life stories to memory; it was their first inter-species friendship. I held up the jar to Nan. "This one is Betty. She wanted to be a concert pianist but wasn't born with the luxury of fingers. And this one," I pointed to another bug, "is Herbert, a bit of an odd duck. Never thought of himself as a potato bug. More of a dragonfly, but try as he might it never stuck. Now he has to content himself with the drudgery of potato buggery." I looked up at Nan. "I don't think they're happy in their glass jar. It's a bit confining, especially when their dreams are so big."

Nan rubbed her temples, as she did during most mealtimes. I think it stimulated her appetite. "They're just bugs, Celia. Nothing more, there are no schemes of grandeur or diabolical regrets."

"How do you know? You've never even talked to a bug, let alone a formidable one."

"I'm glad you have compassion and care for all God's living things, Celia, I really am, but it needs to stretch a little past an Armadillidium vulgare. Perhaps to Mr. Douglas, have you thought of that? He's someone who needs our kindness, whether you realize it or not."

"Does he want to be a concert pianist or a dragonfly?"

"Of course not."

I slumped in my chair. "I find it hard to find sympathy for someone who has less ambition than a potato bug."

CHAPTER 8

GRIGGS DREW the drapes as I set out the pots and pans. "Does she suspect anything?"

I shrugged.

"What did she say when she dropped you off?"

"She told me not to yell at any neighbours."

"What did you do?"

"I made my eyes as big as they could go, as if the very thought of such a thing frightened me."

Griggs grunted and regarded me with her usual amount of suspicion. "Such an arbitrary thing for your Nan to request. Not hollering at the neighbours? Why would you commit to such a thing when you don't know what the day has in store?"

"Exactly," I said.

"Sometimes your Nan is beyond me." The plastic-covered chesterfield crinkled as she took her usual spot. "It's a relief to know that she doesn't suspect anything, and more than that, that you can keep a secret."

I could feel myself puff up. "I keep lots of secrets."

"Name one."

I thought for a moment. "A few weeks back I saw Mr. Douglas's dangling participle."

Griggs sucked her lip. "It's not polite to make things up."

"I'm not, that's what Nan called it."

Griggs didn't say anything, she just got up from her plastic-covered chesterfield and beetled across the room to a bookshelf, picked up a hard-covered dictionary and beetled back.

"Dangling participle, you say?" She plopped back down on the couch, placing the book on her lap. Her nimble fingers leafed through the glued-together pages that thumped from one side of the dark cover to the other. "I don't think it's a word, or even a phrase, to be more precise."

I followed her finger as it ran the length of the page. "It has to be. Nan said it. She never uses made-up words. Maybe it's on one of the stuck-together pages."

Griggs snorted. "That's doubtful. Those words are fit for neither man nor beast. They should have never made their way into the Queen's English. If Shakespeare didn't use them, neither do I. As far as I'm concerned, they don't exist." She ran a finger tenderly down the length of the page before tapping it at the bottom. "Just as I suspected, this time she's wrong." There was a hint of glee in her voice. "Dangling participle, my Aunt Fanny. After all these years, I've got her!"

In celebration, we made our way into the kitchen. Griggs said we could toast her success of finally beating Nan at the Dictionary Game. She took down her orange Tupperware jug and an unopened package of Freshie, one that Griggs hadn't licked around the torn edges.

"You're a tattletale," I said to Griggs, as she stirred the jug of orange liquid.

"How would you know?"

"I heard Nan talking about it, except she didn't say tattletale, she said gossip. She said it was one of the reasons I needed to take everything you say with a grain of salt."

Griggs gave a hard stir with the wooden spoon before filling Mr. Griggs's tall brown Tupperware cup. "A grain of salt," she grunted. "If I had a nickel for every time someone said they should take me with a grain of salt." Her bottom lip quivered. "There is no appreciation in this world for greatness. You say tattletale, I say Town Cryer. They're very different things."

Griggs slapped a Tupperware cup on the table in front of me, causing orange Freshie to slop over its sides onto her checkered tablecloth. Mr. Griggs never raised his button eyes, not wanting to get caught up in the debate.

"That used to be an honoured profession, you know." She filled her own cup before she tapped its side. "Long before your time, long before mine to be truthful, but those were good days. Days when truth was ferreted out, spun and stretched, until it became legendary, like a fine French tapestry."

"Mr. Douglas isn't a tattletale."

"Here we go again. Give it up, Celia. We're not going to talk about his dangling participle, if there is such a thing." She took a sip from her cup before wiping away her orange mustache with the back of her hand. "We were talking about the spreading of indispensable information. Something I've grown very good at, thank you very much. But do you think Oswald Elliot sees any value in it? No. Begged him to share his column and little strip, said I could bring to life all the things he missed. With my colouring skills it would have been epic. He said that such tittle-tattle has fallen out of fashion with polite society. Like he'd know anything about that."

"Doesn't sound much different than what he does."

"Exactly," Griggs rose higher in her seat. "It isn't, it's better. And who am I not to share it with all who are willing to listen?"

I shrugged.

Griggs skid her chrome chair closer to me. "Celia," her chin hooked over my shoulder. "I had a premonition that you were coming over."

"Was that before or after Nan telephoned to ask?"

"It's hard to say, premonitions are a wiggly bunch." She filled my tumbler with more orange Freshie. Like I'd seen in spy movies, she was plying me with her sugary concoction, getting me ready to spill my guts, or make me carry nitro like they did in Gunsmoke. I looked at the glass with a little distrust; I wasn't going to do either.

"Do you think the next time you're out and about, you might let my name slip? Mention me when you're strolling the aisles of the grocery store or passing the collection plate?"

I thought for a moment. It was better than having my arms blown off. "What would I say?"

"Oh, something like, *Mrs. Griggs has the finest spoon collection in Happy Valley,* or *Have you ever seen a finer honeymoon hat?* Something that might catch Oswald Elliot's attention when he's lurking about."

"I suppose, but it might sound a bit awkward. I don't even know what a honeymoon hat is!"

"When has that stopped you before?"

━━━

The next time Nan and me left the house I tried to find a way to mention Griggs's honeymoon hat, but it was hard to fit it into everyday conversation. Up and down the aisles of the Happy Valley's Jolly Grocer I followed my Nan, scratching my head and pondering. It didn't feel like it was something I could slip in while she was riffling through the discount bin of dented cans. Or bring up when she was sniffing the day-old bread. The more I puzzled my predicament, the more daunting it seemed. I didn't want to disappoint Griggs, but I didn't want to irritate Nan either, and I wasn't sure which one was worse.

"What's wrong with you?" Nan asked, as she put away her change purse and picked up her brown paper grocery bag. "You've got worms?"

"No. I was just wondering," I looked around to see if Oswald was anywhere about, "if you had a spoon collection?"

"You know I don't."

"How about a honeymoon hat?"

"No." Nan flushed and pulled the paper grocery bag closer to her chest.

"How come? Was it ugly and that's why you don't want to talk about it?"

Nan turned on her heel. "Sometimes, Celia... Why are you asking?"

There was hurt in her voice. I didn't have the heart to tell her it was Griggs who made me ask; that it was for Oswald Elliot's benefit. "Just curious."

"My advice to you is find something else to be curious about." Nan turned towards home with a pace so brisk you'd have thought her tail was on fire. She didn't even acknowledge Farmer Hempel when he tipped his cap. I apologized for her, explaining she was full of regrets for not having a spoon collection, something she could polish in her spare time while she dreamt of all the places she would never go.

When I caught up with Nan, she had stepped through the screen door and was unpacking the groceries. I made my face go slack; Nan couldn't stay cross at a simpleton.

But no matter how many times I bumped into walls or missed my mouth with spoonfuls of soup, Nan's eyes remained hard.

When I crawled into bed that night I waited in the dark,

listening for her clip-cloppy hard-soled shoes, but she never came.

Even when I made myself accidentally roll out of bed, she didn't rush up to see if I was all right, or call after me. It was the first time she didn't kiss me on the forehead and wish me sweet dreams. That she didn't tell the bugs not to bite me. That she didn't swear I was the best thing that had ever happened to her. It was the first night I tucked myself in.

I couldn't help but wonder if she was downstairs missing my should-have-been ma; kissing her screeching cartoon face on the forehead. Hoping she'd come sashaying up the walk with a basket of wormy fruit, thrown out by the Happy Valley Jolly Grocer. How happy they'd be, my should-have-been ma taking my place at the chrome table. My Nan taking a fine-toothed comb to my should-have-been's rat-infested hair. They'd laugh and Nan would show her where she'd hid the stapler. Then Nan would lean over and slip a strand of hair behind my should-have-been's ear, just like she used to do with me.

I blinked hard. For the first time, I wished I'd never been born.

⸺

The cereal boxes were on the table when I came down to breakfast. Nan was at the kitchen window, looking out towards her garden. I slipped into my chair, lined the bottom of my bowl with a handful of brown sugar, and covered it with a bale of shredded wheat and a slosh of milk. What Nan didn't know wouldn't hurt me.

"Sorry about yesterday, Celia. Sometimes I need time to collect myself." She turned and faced me, and I stuck my hand into the brown sugar bag. Her smile quivered. "You think one handful of sugar is enough?"

"Griggs lets me have two."

"Well, Mrs. Griggs is just trying to hide the taste of milk that has gone off." She pulled up a chair. "What else do you and Mrs. Griggs do?"

I could feel my cheeks grow hot. "I don't know."

"Come now, Celia, there's no reason to be tight-lipped. You haven't been sworn to secrecy, have you?"

"Not exactly."

"What exactly is it then?"

"Griggs says you don't take our pot and pan band seriously. That no matter how hard we practice you'll mock us."

Nan rolled her eyes. "When have I ever mocked you?"

"Right now, maybe."

Without saying another word, Nan watched me finish my breakfast, and then I followed her into the living room. She pulled her latest library book from the stack. "This will do," she said, patting a place beside her on the chesterfield. I snuggled up beside her, sinking into her doughiness. The sweet smell of her was enough to keep me there. But when she opened the cover and started to read, my world expanded.

"*Captain from Castile.*" She licked a finger and turned the page. "*On the evening of June 28, 1518, young Pedro de Vargas, aged nineteen, confessed his sins for the month to Father Juan Mendez. He took them more seriously than the priest, who had been hearing confessions for hours, and was ready for supper. Besides, Father Juan knew the young man so well that he could have guessed beforehand what he would tell him.*"

Pedro and the Spanish inquisition kept us company for most of the morning. Nan and I didn't talk about honeymoon hats or spoon collections. We didn't have to. We were together, keeping company, like we always did. Like I hoped we always would.

CHAPTER 9

IF GOING to Old Lady Griggs's taught me one thing, it was to be prepared. I combed my hair and brushed my teeth without being asked, and when I was finished I'd drag a kitchen chair into the bathroom and examine myself in the mirror. If Oswald Elliot was going to catch me unawares, I'd be ready. "Draw this, Oswald Elliot," I whispered, turning my head this way and that, trying to find my best side. I smiled, grimaced, showed my teeth.

"Celia Canterberry, what are you doing?" Nan stopped short in the bathroom doorway. Her eyebrows were almost touching each other.

I flashed my teeth once more for good measure. "Looking for age spots."

"For the love of Pete, get off that chair before you hurt yourself."

I climbed off the chair, slid it out of the bathroom and back to its spot tucked under the chrome table. By the time I had things put back to rights Nan had poured herself a cup of coffee and was leaning against the kitchen stove. She looked right past me, her eyes somewhere I wasn't. I wanted to ask her what she was thinking about, who she was spending her drifting-around time with. But I wasn't sure I wanted to hear the answer. What if it was with my should-have-been ma? I bit my lip. "What are you wearing to work?" I asked.

Nan glanced down at her dress. "My regular clothes. Why?"

"No reason," I said, giving the chair a final nudge. It wasn't my place to tell her that, if Oswald Elliot and me could do our bit to help with the prosperity of Happy Valley, putting on nylons without stopped-up runs and dabbing on a little lipstick wouldn't kill her. If she spent less time missing my should-have-been and more time on the betterment of her fellow man she'd see these things for herself. All I could do was shake my head.

Nan set down her coffee cup and let out an eye-rolling sigh. "Hold on, Marie Antoinette. Keep your fashion opinions and staplers to yourself." She motioned for me to put on my shoes.

I grunted and did as I was told but I didn't like her attitude. The whole time we walked from Nan's to Griggs's, I wondered if keeping secrets from Nan was the same as her keeping secrets from me, or did adults have different rules than kids? And what would she say if she found out? Would her disappointment in me bubble over so that she'd screech, *You're the same as Audrey!* At the thought I blinked away tears that wouldn't come.

The only thing I could think of doing was to reach up and give Nan's hand a squeeze. She squeezed mine back, same as always. I let out a sigh; maybe it was a sign that Nan knew I was nothing like Audrey. My only fault was looking at scrapbooks, whereas Audrey abandoned babies at hospitals.

"Well, you look better than you did the other day," Griggs said, as she opened her screen door. She said that every time she saw Nan now. Didn't seem to want her to forget her fashion foray into the bizarre and ridiculous.

Nan didn't say anything. She kissed me on the forehead and raised her eyebrows, confident that I'd know what the gesture implied. I didn't have a clue but nodded knowingly. With one last kiss, I slipped from Nan's to Griggs's side.

"What are we going to do today?" I asked.

"That depends," Griggs said, not taking her eyes off Nan, who was walking down the street to the druggist.

"Depends on what?"

"Depends on how much I want to stretch my luck today." She sucked her teeth. "Do you think she suspects?"

I shrugged. "It's hard to tell."

"I know, can't trust that woman as far as I can throw her. She plays her cards too close to her chest. Let your guard down for a minute and she's sure to pounce." Griggs tightened her apron strings. "I think we'll play it safe today."

I didn't know what playing it safe was, until Griggs took a wooden spoon from a kitchen drawer, marched into the living room and plopped down by a gigantic roaster. "Let's see if this band of ours has legs," she said.

I grabbed two pot lids and squatted down beside her. We spent the first ten minutes tuning our instruments. Banging this, clanging that. My heart thrilled inside me and Griggs hummed the whole time. She was enjoying it as much as I was. After a time, Griggs rubbed her temples. "Enough of that. If your Nan was going to check up on us, all this banging would have surely scared her off."

Griggs dusted off her bottom before taking her usual place on her chesterfield. "What haven't I told you about?"

I shrugged. "If you haven't told me, how am I supposed to know?"

"Fair enough. Let's see." She closed her eyes, flicked her fingers and randomly opened the scrapbook. Griggs pointed to the headline. *It Walks*.

"There came a time when your Nan and you could walk down any of Happy Valley's elm-lined streets unimpeded, no one bothering to tip a hat or ask if life was treating you well. As you can well see." Griggs's gnarled finger ran beneath the frames. The images almost moved. "It's hard to tell the difference between the way you waddled then and your Frankenstein-walk now."

"Where were we going?" I asked, a bit concerned. In the comic strip boxes dark storm clouds as far back as the horizon were kicking up dust and almost overturning cars as Nan and I strolled past. The pair of us, holding hands and swinging our arms, were oblivious to the weather that would soon overtake us.

"To Mr. Frank Murray's Haberdashery and Emporium, of course. You couldn't wear clothes made from your Nan's old linen forever. It was the first time you got a set of store-bought clothes."

"Wow." I frowned at the pillowcase with a hole cut for my head and two more for my arms. "Did she really dress me like that?"

"No, of course not. What a foolish question. It was all quite logical, cotton for summer, flannel for winter. And she never used her best pillowcases; that one's not even patched." Griggs waved a dismissive hand before she began to read. *Celia Canterberry stumbles from her winter captivity, a wildcat out of hibernation. Children run for cover while grown men hide in their household cupboards or behind their mothers' skirts. It is the beginning of the end.*

A row of cartoon boxes showed me and Nan making our way down the street. The closer we got to our destination, the longer my fingernails grew, while my baby teeth turned into fangs. Nan let go of my hand and I began staggering to and fro, frothing at the mouth. Even Nan looked frightened.

Mrs. Whitford, heavy with child, grasps the cross around her neck as a small devil-child makes its way toward her. Her husband, momentarily distracted by his reflection in his brand new pharmacy's storefront window, hears his beloved's anguished cry and throws her to the ground, covering her expansive frame with his own.

At that moment Agnes Obermeyer exits the newly reopened Happy Valley Druggist, her arms full of supplies. Staplers, thumb tacks, reams of paper, permanent Jiffy markers, anything that a God-appointed mayor might be in need of. She almost trips over the prostrate couple. "That's love," Agnes coos, as she drops her materials and bends to wipe a trickle of blood escaping a fresh gash on Mrs. Whitford's forehead. "I wish someone cared that much for me."

"If wishes were horses," Mrs. Whitford manages from under her husband's bulk, "beggars would ride."

Griggs stopped reading. "Don't be fooled," she said. "That druggist doesn't care one whit for his wife. As soon as he married her the honeymoon was over. He was just after someone to pay off some gambling debts and front him the money to buy a business, and Enid fit the bill. Her father would have paid almost anything to get her off his hands. Besides, throwing his wife to the ground was the only way he could seem heroic and save his new suit pants from being soiled when he dropped to the ground himself."

"Where's the love in that?"

"Exactly." Griggs got all puffed up and said she was thankful that Mr. Griggs was not inclined to toss her around. Although when she mentioned that fact to Mrs. Whitford, the other scoffed and said that Mr. Griggs wasn't good for much, never was, even before he became a permanent fixture at her kitchen table. "I'll never forgive her for that," Griggs said.

I took a breath and let Griggs stew for a while before I tapped a finger on the comic strip. In the box, the devil child was gnawing on some boy's arm.

"You must recognize who that is," Griggs said.

I shook my head and Griggs started up again.

The O'Reilly twins, both destined for the priesthood, amble down the streets of Happy Valley, eyes agog with wonder. The storm that had been drummed up by the presence of the Canterberrys dissipates under the serene influence of the O'Reillys. The boys could calm the waters of Galilee. A more innocent pair never graced the streets of Happy Valley.

I interrupted Griggs. "Is there another set of O'Reilly twins?"

"No, just the one."

"I've never seen that pair. They're clean." My eyes scanned the page. Oswald Elliot had drawn me as the town ghoul and he'd drawn the O'Reillys as if they'd been dipped in bleach. They glowed in their goodness. It didn't make sense.

"They stole those clothes from the storefront window of Murray's Haberdashery," Griggs said. "Right in the middle of the day when Mr. Murray was taking a nap in the back room. Allowing the 'down and going' to enter through the same door as the 'up and coming' didn't go over very well with The Ladies of the Perpetual Indigence Society. They have their standards, and would have disapproved of his lapsed gatekeeping. The only thing he could do was bite his tongue and let the O'Reillys get off scot-free."

From what I knew of the O'Reillys, most days they spent their time skulking around town, their crusty fingers digging in some gutter for half-smoked cigarette butts. They weren't 'up and coming,' even with their clothes all pressed and matching. The O'Reilly twins weren't the pressed or matching types; they were destined for prison stripes. They'd set enough fires in Happy Valley to rival Armageddon, and that was when they were feeling charitable.

"Nan said the only place the O'Reilly twins are headed for is the Happy Valley Penitentiary. She says if those two used the good sense God gave them, they'd get their penitentiary numbers before all the good ones are gone, or someone less deserving claims them. The sooner they do, the sooner the digits can be retired."

Griggs nodded. "You're preaching to the choir, sister. And let me tell you, that family's fall from grace can't all be blamed on one little bite." Her lazy eye narrowed. "Don't let it trouble you too much."

Up until that point it hadn't been troubling me, because I had no idea what Griggs was talking about. "What little bite?"

"Don't you remember?"

"No."

"Oh, it was the talk of the town, how the oldest O'Reilly twin bent down to bless you and you clamped on to his arm with the jaws of a bear trap. Your Nan could hardly pry you off. There was so much blood, at least the way Oswald drew it there was. I, once again, wasn't there." Griggs let out a heart-wrenching sigh. "According to Happy Valley legend, that's the day the O'Reillys turned."

I looked down at the comic strip. It was hard to believe I was a biter, and that I could turn good children bad. I wanted to ask Nan if I was the only one, or if I came from a long line of biters. That would explain a lot.

"No one blames you." Griggs tilted her head. "Well, I suppose that's a bit of an overstatement. No one in this *house* blames you. I can't speak for the rest of Happy Valley. Well anyways, the whole town thought when Mrs. O'Reilly got the stigmata that all the fire-starting would stop — that your bite had been annulled. But I could have told them, I tried, God knows I tried, that the whole thing was a ruse. I knew it the first time I saw Mrs. O'Reilly traipse around town in those white gloves. Those gloves with the splotchy red that oozed through the fabric on the palm."

"The stigmata," I repeated, as if I knew the word, but Nan hadn't introduced me to it yet in the Dictionary Game.

"It didn't take long for me to confirm my suspicion that it was fake," Griggs explained. "It was a couple of years back during Easter service. I was exhausted from lugging Mr. Griggs up and down the aisle because the O'Reillys kept moving each time we got close. When the Reverend insisted the game of musical chairs was over, and it was time to take our seats, the O'Reillys had no choice. I slipped into the seat beside Mrs. O'Reilly, and I'm sure I don't have to tell you that it was a bit awkward.

"Mr. Griggs hadn't been out in public for some time, and there were so many who wanted to wish him well, so I was quite spent. I had to catch my breath before I could prop him up with a hymnal in his lap. I was just about to bend over to tie my shoe when Mr. Griggs shifted beside me. He was beginning to slide out of the pew. It was his gout, poor man; it brings him to his knees. I repositioned him, and gave him a sharp look by way of a warning. This was no time to give in to his proclivities."

I nodded and looked towards the kitchen; I didn't want to be overheard by Mr. Griggs. "What does any of this have to do with Mrs. O'Reilly's stigmata?"

"Hold your horses, young lady, I'm getting to that." Griggs frowned. "I was just setting the scene." She templed her fingers, tapping the tips together. "As I was saying, I bent to tie my shoe. And when I was in that vulnerable position, I twitched my head deliberately so that my honeymoon hat caught in her hosiery. I'd stuck extra pins backwards in it for that very purpose earlier that morning. They poked out like the arms of a starfish."

"Makes sense," I said, but it was a lie. None of what Griggs did made much sense to me.

"Exactly," she said, slapping me on the leg. "In a different time, we could have been spies. Can you imagine me and Mr.

Griggs, in our trench coats and pointed shoes, slipping in and out of shadows, passing secret messages to unshaven strangers?"

"What about Mr. Griggs's gout?"

She raised an eyebrow. "Good spies don't have gout. Don't you know anything about subterfuge?" She paused. "Where was I?"

"The pins in your honeymoon hat."

"Oh yes. As Mrs. O'Reilly reached down to free her ruined hosiery, I licked the palm of her gloved hand." If Griggs had had a moustache, she'd have twirled it. "Ketchup!" she cried triumphantly.

"Ketchup?"

"Yes, that's what I said. Mrs. O'Reilly doesn't have the stigmata. She's just unwashed."

Having the stigmata may have been beyond my grasp, but unwashed hands were an everyday occurrence for me. Griggs could have been a spy. I admired her more than ever.

Old Lady Griggs beamed about her honeymoon hat and Easter espionage. "That nasty O'Reilly woman just wanted to get her own comic book strip. Toss you and your Nan over as if all your strangeness accounted for nothing."

"Unbelievable! The nerve of some people." I shook my head. "So, did I turn the O'Reilly boys to a life of crime, or were they headed in that direction anyway?"

Griggs fixed me with her ambitious eye. "You shall know the tree by its fruit, my dear."

Exactly what I was afraid of.

CHAPTER 10

WHEN NAN PICKED me up at Griggs's, she wasn't very chatty, and only nodded to Mr. Griggs instead of greeting him properly. "It's been a long day," she said. "And it's not even halfway over."

Griggs grunted. "We can't all have important lives like you."

"Being overwhelmed isn't the mark of an important life. It's a mark of a poverty-stricken one."

"Well, you said it. I didn't."

Nan rolled her eyes and held a hand towards me. "We'll see you tomorrow, Dorigen."

"If you're not too busy."

"I'll check my schedule," Nan called over her shoulder.

We were halfway back to Nan's when she turned to me. "Celia," she said, "I know things have been trying since I've taken on a job at the Happy Valley Druggist. I've had less energy, and God knows less patience."

I nodded.

"So I've decided to give you the afternoon off. No spritzing for you today." Her voice was light and airy, like this was a good thing.

"Not so fast," I said. "Spritzing is one of my favourite things."

"Are you sure?"

I let out a long breath. How could she even ask? That's when we both got to stand around and guess *Whose stain was it, anyway?* I learned all kinds of things from spritzing. "See this spot here?" Nan would say. I'd bend over and shake my head. "Well there used to be a spot there," Nan would explain. "I thought I would have to scrub it until doomsday. Nasty little thing."

"How did it get there?" I'd say.

"What do you think?"

I'd wrinkle my brow and tap a finger on my chin. "It's Mrs. Murray? It looks like something she'd wear." Nan would nod. "Maybe," I'd say, "in a drunken stupor she climbed a tree to check out a bird's nest. The nest of a bird that was soon to be extinct."

"I doubt that," Nan would say. "She's a teetotaler. And hates the Happy Valley avifauna." "Maybe," I'd say, filing that one away for later, "she was running away from the 'down and goings' and tripped."

"Perhaps," Nan would reply.

We could go on like that for hours, but now Nan wanted me to give the whole thing up? Like it wasn't one of our favourite pastimes? One little stain could change the way a girl looked at the world.

Nan smiled as she hummed her way into her house. "I think you will change your mind."

"Fat chance," I mumbled.

The lunch dishes had barely been cleared away when we heard a knock on the screen door. Nan hunched her shoulders and waggled her eyebrows, like a knock wasn't an everyday occurrence. As she investigated, I spritzed the air, feeling the mist of the water droplets on my face. "I miss you, my lovelies," I whispered. That's when I heard the voice. It was Mrs. Quigley, although she didn't go by Quigley anymore. The woman was always getting married; Griggs said she needed a Rosetta Stone just to cipher which Mrs. she was at the moment. It didn't matter to me; my heart skipped all the way up to my throat. Mrs. Quigley was my best friend Archibald's mother. I hadn't seen Archibald since her mother, Mrs. Whoever-She-Was now, had picked her up on the last day of Grade One. They were headed to Archibald's grandparents – the parents of one of her long-gone fathers – and now they'd come back without me even hearing about it.

"I appreciate this, Molly," I heard her say. "I shouldn't be gone for more than an hour."

Nan opened the screen door and Archibald stepped inside. She looked as brown as a berry. I ran to her and threw my arms around her, dreaming of all the adventures we'd have together now that she was back. She squealed like a baby goat, just like the first day of Grade One. "My cup runneth over," I said.

"So does mine," Archibald whispered back. She wasn't just my best friend, she was better than that. She was my earthworm friend.

The first time I laid eyes on Archibald she was standing outside Griggs's house. Her mother had gone inside to return Old Lady Griggs's uneaten condolence casserole. I was stirring mud puddles and minding my own business. Once I'd finished stirring and rescuing in one puddle, I adjusted my bolty neck and Frankenstein-walked to the next. Without even asking, Archibald adjusted her own bolty neck and joined me. Her Frankenstein-hands sifted through the muddy water, saving as many worms as I did. It was a thing of beauty. From that day forward we'd been inseparable, until she'd left to visit her grandparents.

"Celia," Nan said, interrupting our reunion. "Do you hear me?"

I nodded, even though I didn't have a clue what she was talking about. I was too busy glorying in Archibald. Stretching out our arms and adjusting our bolty necks, Archibald and me Frankenstein-walked through the kitchen, up the stairs, and into my bedroom. Archibald had never been to my house. She looked around before plopping down on my bed. "Must be pretty quiet here," she said. "Since there is just you and no other kids to fight with."

I shrugged. "I suppose," letting my words drag out as I closed the door. "Never really thought about it. Been too busy keeping secrets." I sat next to her nonchalantly and let the words sink in. If Archibald was a cat she'd be dead at least half a dozen times. She poked her nose in to almost everything she caught wind of.

She leaned forward. "What secrets?"

I let out a sigh so she would know the whole experience was weighing on me. I didn't want to tell her my secret worry of kids sticking their erasers in my empty eye sockets. Scientifically, it was too hard to explain. So, after another sigh I got straight to the point; I didn't want to take too long. When Nan had been giving me my polite host instructions, I recalled her saying we only had an hour. I assumed whatever else she'd gone on about had to do with matches or chewing gum. "Griggs told me not to tell."

"Who aren't you suppose to tell?"

"Nan."

"I'm not your Nan."

She had a point. I flopped back on the bed. "Oswald Elliot has made my life into a comic book strip."

Archibald wrinkled her brow. "Is that all?" she said. "Everyone knows that."

"How come no one told me?"

She hunched one shoulder. "Scared of your Nan, I bet. My mom said she almost lost her mind when she found out. Threatened to burn down city hall. I think the whole incident made it into the comic strip."

"Griggs hasn't shown me that one."

"I'm not surprised. Has she shown you mine?"

"Your what?"

"My comic strip."

I could feel myself stiffen. "*Your* comic strip?"

"Yup, Oswald's been drawing it since I was a baby."

"Has not!"

"Has so."

"Has not." I was starting to wish that lying Archibald had stayed at her out-of-town grandparents'. I leaned over and gave her hair a tug. Not enough to pull it from its roots, but enough to let her know I wasn't pleased. She tugged mine back, harder.

"What did you do that for?" I said, a little shocked that she could be so discourteous.

"You did it first."

"That was my prerogative."

"It was my prerogative too."

I rolled my eyes; this was going nowhere.

Archibald blinked back a tear. "I don't care if you roll your eyes, I don't care if you don't believe me. It's true. Ask Mrs. Griggs. She says it might win the Pulitzer Surprise."

That was a bridge too far. It was all I could do not to grab two handfuls of her hair and drag her to the floor.

Archibald tightened her lips and looked past me, as if we had never been friends at all. I sat up and crossed my arms, and she did the same, neither of us speaking to one another. Having a friend over to play was no fun at all. How dare Archibald act like my comic strip wasn't special? That everyone and their dog had one. I wanted to spit in her eye.

When Nan came upstairs to tell Archibald it was time to go home, I pretended to be asleep. Archibald stomped out as soon as the door was open. "Are you ready, honey?" I heard Nan ask as they slipped down the hall.

"I've been ready for a long time," Archibald grumbled.

I was still mad when Nan called me for supper.

"Did you and Archibald have a nice time?" Nan laid a napkin on her lap.

"I suppose," I lied.

"There is no supposing about it, you either did or you didn't."

"I don't feel good," I said. "May I be excused?"

Nan leaned over and put the back of her hand to my forehead. "You're not hot." Her eyes searched mine. "But if you're sure you're not feeling well, you may be excused."

Nodding, I stomped all the way to my room. Griggs was going to hear about this.

CHAPTER 11

THAT NIGHT I couldn't fall asleep. I tossed and turned, trying to get my disappointment with Archibald to simmer down. I had never been so disappointed in anyone in my entire life, bragging about having her own comic strip when I was divulging my deepest, darkest secret. What kind of earthworm friend would do that? I flipped through my Archibald memories. A little to my disappointment, they were all delightful, not one hinting at her recent treachery. The more I flipped, the more confused I got. How was I supposed to stay mad at her? It would be exhausting. Who else would notice if it was good earthworm weather? To soothe myself I closed my eyes, and I sank into my favourite Archibald memory: the first day of school.

That day Nan took a long time to get ready, even fishing out a wobbly tube of lipstick from the bottom of her purse. The tube she saved for weddings and going to the big city.

"How do I look?" she'd said, as she turned around in front of her cracked bedroom mirror.

"About the same as you did two changes ago."

She frowned. "You're no help."

I shrugged, wasn't trying to be. All her fussing was making me anxious. I paced around blowing out my cheeks and trying not to come out of my skin. It was no use. In exasperation I flopped down on Nan's bed and waited for her to yell at me for mussing it up. She didn't even notice. I sprawled out, tracing the lines in her tufted chenille bedspread; every once in a while, I pulled out one of those tiny colourful threads. After they were pulled, I had no choice, I had to devour the evidence; thought it might calm me.

"This will have to do," Nan said, without noticing what I was doing. She reached for her church gloves and best handbag.

That combination made me sit straight up and widen my eyes. "Those are your Sunday gloves, but we're not going to church."

"Sometimes one needs to make an impression." Nan leaned over and tweaked my nose. Her eyebrows knit together as the bedspread caught her attention. "That's strange," she said, bending over and running a hand over the covering. "I swear those bare patches weren't here when I made my bed this morning."

Flopping back down, I placed my elbows on the bed, and tucked my chin daintily in the palms of my hands. "Mice," I said very matter of a fact. "Only thing it could be."

Nan straightened and sniffed the air, her eyes scanning this way and that. "Can't be, there aren't any droppings."

"Constipated I bet, considering all those little fine threads packed tight in their bloating insides. Lucky for you one didn't burst open and die under your pillow. That's what happened to Mrs. Griggs; they chewed right through her honeymoon nightie. Said it exposed her to all kinds of ridicule."

"I suppose you're right. We should be off." She pulled herself away from the puzzling mystery of the chenille spread. "There are bigger fish to fry at the *Happy Valley School for Reluctant Children*."

The way she said *reluctant children* sounded like a threat. I could feel the hair on the back of my neck stir when Nan offered me her hand. I only took it in hopes that she'd forget about her tufted chenille bedspread and the bare patches that marred it. Once we were out of the house, I was filled with relief. This was the start of a new adventure. I skipped and sang at the top of my lungs, and although Nan stiffened from time to time, she didn't stop me. It wasn't until we reached the *Happy Valley School for Reluctant Children* that I stopped short.

"Aptly named, don't you think?" Nan said, pulling up beside me.

My eyes shifted from the school to the *Happy Valley Penitentiary*. The buildings were only a stone's throw apart. Mayor Forde had said it was best that way; it saved money on the chain-link fence. Nan wasn't as pragmatic, although she said it was easier for some of Happy Valley's less fortunate families; drop the kids off at school and kiss your husband good morning in one fell swoop. I looked towards the fence as the men pressed against it and wondered which one was Mayor Forde's brother-in-law.

"Don't worry," Nan said squeezing my hand a bit harder. "That razor wire keeps most of them on their own side of the fence."

I squeezed back, taking a deep breath as we picked up our pace, but I couldn't help looking over my shoulder from time to time just to make sure. Once we stepped through the school doors the excitement overtook me. I'd never seen so many children in one place. The halls were full of pushers and shovers; I knew in an instant I'd fit right in. I let go of Nan's hand and looked around. Who would I shove first? There were so many possibilities. Decisions, decisions. That's when I caught the attention of Billy Billboson's mother. She stepped between me and Billy as if she could read my mind. I let my face go slack, while Billy Billboson's mother licked two thick fingers and petted the top of Billy's rather bulbous head, making his three strands of hair — Larry, Moe and Curly — lay flat. To a child, we all stood in wonder.

Mrs. Billboson's petting soothed the bombastic cranium, and Billy was soon all droopy-eyed and saggy-shouldered. "This too shall pass," she said, her voice all simperingly sweet.

Nan snorted and raised her chin higher in the air, which caused Mrs. Billboson to increase her petting with such vigour I thought Larry, Moe, and Curly would get worn right through. Luckily for the trio, Mrs. Hoopenmire diverted Mrs. Billboson's aberrant attention.

"See over there?" she said in a whisper so loud that I was sure it could be heard at the penitentiary. "Shelly Shepard's mother didn't even trim that little moustache of hers, let alone shave it." She gave an indignant sniff. "And it's the first day of school, you'd think she'd want to make an impression."

"She did," Mrs. Billboson chortled, which set the wattle under her chin wobbling uncontrollably, causing a draft that stirred Billy's hairs. "What other girl in the first grade can say she's well on her way to having a handlebar moustache?"

"Oh, not many I'm sure." Mrs. Hoopenmire pulled her own little oddity closer. Lenard Hoopenmire, her youngest, was hard to miss; in the right light, he seemed to be a striking shade of green. The Hoopenmires lived by an old paint factory, and it was no secret that Mrs. Hoopenmire couldn't stop Lenard from drinking the glowing neon water.

Mrs. Shepard turned on the pair. "I'll have you know we come from a long line of circus performers, and facial hair runs in our blood, like talent." She glanced dismissively at Billy's naked melon. "Not even enough for a decent comb-over."

Nan and I stood there watching the three women, trying to be invisible. I thought it was a good time to practice being simpletons, but knew Nan would have none of it. Even so, it was hard to be an invisible simpleton when Nan was wearing her forest green and florescent pink Fortrel sheath dress. When the group turned on us, I knew Nan felt it had been a mistake as well. She tugged at her dress as her cheeks flushed.

"Well," Mrs. Hoopenmire said, looking the pair of us up and down, "I didn't expect to see the two of you here."

"And why not?" Nan gave her dress a final tug, forcing a band of fabric from a roll where it had been exploring her underbelly. "Celia has just as much right to be here as any of yours." She scanned the others' offspring and sighed.

"Never said she didn't, but with the penitentiary so close, we thought you might skip this step." Mrs. Shepard gave her best Sunday smile while her daughter fingered her moustache. "You know what they say? A stitch in time saves nine."

"I'm sure it does," Nan said, placing her hands firmly on my shoulders. "But we're not talking about stitching, are we? We're talking about the education of our children, and you must all agree an education trumps ignorance?"

There was no response, so Nan continued. "That's why I'm here, to assure Celia gets the best education possible, despite what obstacles may lay ahead." Nan's gentle tirade was cut short when I caught sight of Archibald Quigley. She squealed and began to Frankenstein-walk towards me. I adjusted my bolty neck and let loose my draggy leg, meeting her halfway in the crowded hallway.

When I limped past Timmy he shrieked and piddled before pulling his mother's blousy skirt over his head.

The whole thing might have gone unnoticed, as it was hard to tell he'd had an accident in his checkered polyester pants, but Miss Dobbs came clicking out of her classroom to see what all the fuss was about. She was in her make-a-good-impression pencil skirt, which hampered the speed of her investigation. She slipped in Timmy Crybaby-Head's puddle, ripping open one of the form-fitting seams, exposing a good part of her Playtex Living Girdle.

I winked at Archibald. I was learning so much. To my mind, it was a rather good start to my first day at school.

CHAPTER 12

IN THE MORNING, I'd come to shaky terms with Archibald, but not Griggs. She'd been keeping things from me. I told Nan I could walk to Griggs' by myself, knowing she would just hold me back. "All right," she said, as I zoomed past her. "Be good."

I made no promises.

Old Lady Griggs was sitting at her kitchen table taking the curlers out of her hair when I came barreling in. "Did you wipe your feet?" she asked. "I don't need you traipsing in God knows what from God knows where."

I looked over my shoulder. "There's no mat to wipe my feet on."

"Oh, that's right." Griggs dropped a curler into her overnight bag. "Mr. Douglas's mangy cat threw up on it. Told him he had to buy me a new one. Not going to scrub my fingers to the bone trying to get out rat innards." She looked me up and down. "You can wipe your feet twice tomorrow."

I gave a slight nod before I got to the point. "Archibald says she has a comic strip."

Griggs's lazy eye wobbled. "Why were you and Archibald talking about comic strips?"

"That's not important."

"Yes, it is."

"Archibald is my friend," I said, as my face heated up. "What kind of friend would I be if I told you she brought the whole thing up and started bragging? How are you to think well of her then?"

"You are a wonder," Griggs said, taking my hand and giving it a squeeze. "She's lucky to have you in her life."

I nodded. Not many would have pulled her hair so lightly.

Griggs drew a long breath. "It's like this: once a year or so, when she's getting close to her due date — I think she's going by Mrs. Willoughby now — Oswald puts Canterberry Tales on a hiatus and dusts off *The Deadman's Wife*. Just before the black widow has her baby, and Archibald gets a new sibling, her husband dies, Oswald publishes his scoop, and then the excitement dissipates. When he comes to his senses, Oswald returns to *Canterberry Tales*."

"Do you think..." I couldn't bring myself to say it.

"*The Deadman's Wife?*"

I nodded. "Has a chance to win the Pulitzer Surprise?"

"Not a chance. Not if you have anything to do with it."

"So why did you tell Archibald it did?"

"The girl had just lost another father. I had to say something to cheer her up." Griggs took out her last curler and finger combed her hair. "I don't think you have anything to worry about. On the surface, a whole family of Little Orphan Annies would be hard to compete with, but you have the town's contempt — at least your should-have-beens do. And contempt trumps pity every time."

For the first time in my life it felt good to have people despising me.

By the time Griggs pulled out the scrapbook, it was a whole different experience. It wasn't just about discovering my past, it was about outdoing Archibald Quigley, my best friend and nemesis.

Leaning my head on Griggs's shoulder, I said, "When Archibald came over to play yesterday I lied to her."

"Did she deserve to be lied to?"

"Yes ma'am. She said a lady at church had her autograph one of *The Deadman's Wife* strips. Said that they thought she was the cutest thing standing next to that cartoon coffin."

"What did you tell her?"

"I said, 'That's nothing, one day I was sitting in church by that old plastic pearls and bouffant hairdo lady, the one who passes out every Easter when they talk about nailing Jesus to the cross.'"

"Mrs. Fernsby," interjected Griggs.

I wrinkled my nose.

"That's her name."

"Anyways, Archibald's eyes went wide. She said nobody in their right mind would sit by that woman on purpose, she faints like clockwork. That's when I told my second lie. The first was that I sat by Mrs. Fernsby, the second was that I spoke to her. I said me and Mrs. Fernsby were talking about *Canterberry Tales* and how she'd made it into last month's strip. I told her she'd looked rather fetching in her chipped pearls and bouffant hairdo. And she'd said, 'So glad you noticed. I've taking a liking to that sketch. Have it hanging in my living room right next to a picture of Jesus being stabbed with a spear. I can't go into that room now without passing out.'"

Griggs was quiet for a while. "Did Archibald believe you?"

"It's hard to say, with all the grunting and hair pulling."

"Well, a little hair pulling never hurt anyone." Griggs patted my leg.

I sighed and snuggled deeper into Griggs. What a wonderful way to spend the morning.

CHAPTER 13

THE NEXT MORNING, Nan's day off, I was perched on Nan's dresser, smelling her cold cream and powder puffing my armpits, which I had to admit was one of my favourite pastimes. Nan was taking a bath and had left me to my own devices. To be honest, those weren't her exact words; she thought I was still asleep. Anyway, I was just about to plunge a finger into her exotic Avon cream, when out of the corner of my eye I saw movement through the window. Standing straight up, I catapulted myself off the dresser and onto the centre of Nan's springy bed. From there I slid to the floor and rolled to the window, lifting my head so my eyes were barely peeking above the window ledge. Just as I suspected, Sneaky Walker was poking around Nan's caragana hedge for the second time this week, except this time Tiberius wasn't by his side. I scratched my head. How many rats could one man eat?

I hadn't brought Sneaky Walker up since the rodent incident, but now that he was roaming around the front yard like he owned the place, it gave me reason to reconsider the situation.

"Sneaky Walker's here," I said to Nan, as she walked into her room wrapped in a bath towel. I slid on my belly to the other side of the windowsill, peeking over its edge. "He's snooping in our bushes."

Nan stopped in the doorway. If she'd gained even a thimble of peace in her bathtub soak, it drained from her face now. "What have you done?"

"Nothing," I said from my crouched position. "I've been watching, not yelling or throwing things."

"What's that white powder in your armpits?"

"Oh that," I said, a little disappointed in myself for forgetting I was wearing my spaghetti strap dress. The sweater that I'd put on earlier that morning was on the floor in front of Nan's dresser. If I was going to be a successful spy, I'd have to remember where I dropped my clothing. "I woke up that way," I said, a look of wonder on my face.

Nan rolled her eyes and pointed me out of her room. I Quasimodo-walked my way out the door. I thought it would please her, him being a character from one of her favourite books, but there was no discernible response.

When Nan emerged from her bedroom, I was waiting for her. My sweater was buttoned to its collar and I'd pulled on my red rubber boots.

"What's going on?" she asked, looking down at my footwear.

"Sneaky Walker is still outside." I was starting to feel exasperated; my boots should have been self-evident.

"Don't call him that. His name is Mr. Douglas." Nan lifted my chin with one finger. "The boots?"

"In case we have to chase him through a slough."

"There will be no slough-chasing today. If he's in the bushes, it's because he's looking for Tiberius. He came by last night, said the poor cat was missing and asked if I had seen him."

"Have you?"

"No," she said. "If I had, I'd have locked the windows and barred the doors."

"Oh," I said. "That's a relief. The chicken we had last night for supper was a little gamey."

Mr. Douglas, that Sneaky Walker, was still rummaging through the bushes when Nan and I sat down to breakfast. "I think it's best you don't go outside," she said. "You'll only upset Mr. Douglas, and he doesn't need to worry about you and his cat at the same time."

"That's not fair. Why should a mangy old cat keep me housebound?"

"Because I said so."

I curled my lip. "That animal is unnatural, even Old Lady Griggs says so. She says he changes colour with the sun. In the morning he's black, by lunch he's brown, and when the moon comes out, he's silvery. She's seen the two of them prowl around the neighbourhood as if they're looking for their next meal. Hiding in her wash line, jumping out of piles of junk when unsuspecting innocents pass by, Tiberius sinking his claws in until they can shake him off."

Nan didn't say anything. She sipped her coffee as if she didn't have a thought in her head. Picking up the cereal box, I dug my hand to the bottom to fish out the prize. "Griggs says the way that cat looks at folks it's like it wants to lick the skin right off their bones. Even Sneaky Walker's arms are all scarred from him. I hope Farmer Hempel runs him over with his tractor."

Nan's head snapped to attention, and her gaze became so focused, I thought her glare would burn right through me. "Celia," she said. "You know better than to talk like that. Mr. Douglas loves that cat, and it's not for you or me to wish ill of it."

I picked up my glass of milk. "I wasn't wishing, I was hoping." They were very different things, but I didn't think Nan appreciated the nuance.

"Honestly, Celia, who do you think straightened your bike tire when you ran into the side of the shed for the umpteenth time?"

"It wasn't on purpose."

"I never said it was. But who do you think?"

I didn't say anything.

"And who do you think rototilled the garden this spring while we were in church?"

I shrugged.

"I think, Miss Swiss," Nan's eyes widened, her tone devoid of any pleasantness, "it's a play in your room day."

"Why?"

"I think you know why. Be kind!"

The sun was shining, butterflies were fluttering about, and I was stuck inside. It was a cruel and unusual punishment. Nan had taken away the stapler, and I hadn't seen a pair of scissors since that day at the Happy Valley Druggist. I'd be bored in minutes. "What about Old Lady Griggs? Can she come over?"

The look on Nan's face was one I'll never forget. I might as well have told her I didn't want her to be my Nan anymore, or that I thought the Dictionary Game was stupid. She narrowed her eyes. The thought of me wanting to spend my day with Griggs seemed to infuriate her, and she sent me to my room with only the stupid cereal box prize to occupy me; a sticker of some ditsy cartoon girl, no less. At least *Canterberry Tales* had some gravitas.

As soon as I was in my room I shut the door. My imagination shuffled through a heap of ideas; images swam out of the pages of the stories Nan had read me.

I looked around. My bed seemed the best place to start. I hooked one end of my sheet to the curtain rod and the other to my headboard; the makeshift rigging of a sailboat. First, I was Queequeg chasing a whale, then I was Franz from Swiss Family

Robinson, avoiding rocks in the perilous sea. When I tired of that, I slipped under my bed and pulled down the blankets until there wasn't a bit of light. I was Huw, from How Green Was My Valley. I lay there, counting the bed springs by feel. Huw had a dismal existence.

It was only a matter of time before hunger set in, so I lifted out my heat rad cover and played big game hunter. From that register hole anything could pop up. I hovered over the opening, brandishing a hairbrush, but it didn't matter how long I waited, nothing but a hairball emerged, wafting up on a draft from the kitchen. I patted it on its brave little head and promised to find him a dust bunny to play with. Sitting cross-legged, I looked in a box at the bottom of my closet. Cardboard dolls with their bright paper dresses did little to entice me. Archibald said a mind could snap if one played with those little beauties for too long; Griggs being the prime example. I wasn't playing paper dolls, but I was snapping. "What to do, what to do?"

Then it came to me. I pushed aside my sail, stood on my bed, and slid up the window. "Hey, Sneaky Walker. Find your mangy cat and go home. I want to go outside and play."

Nan was in my room so quick I didn't have time to climb down from my sailboat bed.

"You are going to apologize," she barked.

My mouth went dry. "I never said it. Queequeg did."

"Well, put on your peg leg and let's go."

"Queequeg doesn't have a peg leg; that's Captain Ahab."

Nan sighed at the ceiling. "So sorry for confusing my whalers."

"I accept your apology," I said, straightening the sail. Then I lowered my voice, so it was syrupy sweet, without a hint of condescension. "Now that wasn't so hard was it?"

Nan grabbed me by the ear and marshalled me out of the house. My fairy-hand-wings flapped almost imperceptibly as I fluttered to keep up with her. Now I was Puck. And Nan, well, she was Oberon. Oberon has trouble being reasonable.

She pulled up short in front of Mr. Douglas, that Sneaky Walker. He was standing in front of the biggest elm tree in town, and there, right beneath it, was his mangy cat.

"He's treed something." Mr. Douglas shaded his eyes with a hand as he looked up into the branches. "But I can't tell what it is."

Nan followed Mr. Douglas's gaze. "With those plaid pants, it can only be one person. Oswald Elliot."

I almost fainted on the spot. Oswald Elliot sightings, in my estimation, were rarer than hen's teeth. Peering up into the branches, I wondered how much of me he could see. Was I as hard to make out as he was? How would he sketch me, all forlorn staring up into the abyss, if he couldn't see my forlornness? I cleared my throat, throwing my arms wide. "A spoon collection, a spoon collection, my kingdom for a spoon collection." I fell defeated to my knees, my face searching the heavens.

"Oh, Celia really?" Without warning, Nan picked up a stone and threw it into the branches, beaning Oswald Elliot. He hollered like he'd been shot. I dropped my arms and started searching for a stone of my own.

"No, Celia," Nan said. "The man's defenceless."

"You did it."

"I was checking to see if he was still alive."

"Maybe I want to check too."

"There's no need to. A dead man can't yammer like that. Besides, you know why we're here." She glanced over at Mr. Douglas and coughed discreetly.

My fairy-hand-wings fluttered, and I felt suspended, not knowing which way to dart. Nan grabbed hold of my ear and gave it another tug. My suspension vanished. "Mr. Douglas," I said, as Puckishly as I could, "Nan seems to think I've said something to upset you."

Mr. Douglas frowned. "I'm not upset."

It was all I could do not to turn to Nan and say *I told you so*, but she beat me to the punch. She placed a hand on Sneaky Walker's arm as if it was something she did every day. "Let her finish, Walter; she needs the practice. God knows she needs the practice."

I flapped my fairy wings in protest. Why would I need to practice something that even Sneaky Walker didn't want me to do? I stopped fluttering when Sneaky Walker bent over, put his hands on his knees, and brought his face inches from mine. I could have burped on him. Wrinkling my nose, I thought if I was Puck and Nan was Oberon, then Sneaky Walker was Cobweb. He'd make the perfect Cobweb; the mere thought made me like him better. "Mr. Douglas," I said with a curtsy, "I don't know if you heard —"

"The whole neighbourhood heard," Nan interrupted, reaching for my ear. "And if you don't get to the point, I can think of a long list of chores for you to do, and believe me, you won't like any of them."

I cleared my throat and started again. "It has come to my attention there might be a misunderstanding. If you heard me say, 'Hey, Sneaky Walker, find your mangy cat and go home. I want to go outside and play,' that's not what I meant. I meant, 'Yoo-hoo, Mr. Douglas. Hope you find Tiberius, that wonderful kitten. Have a nice day.'" I did another curtsy.

Mr. Douglas nodded and straightened, arching his back when he did.

"That wasn't much of an apology." Nan jabbed me in the back with a sharp finger.

"None needed," Mr. Douglas said. "I didn't hear a thing."

I smiled. He was making such a good Cobweb. Cobweb the

Sneaky Walker. Shakespeare himself would have kissed him on his pate. I wanted to tell him but knew Nan would just make me apologize again. How could I explain that we were all characters from some play that Cobweb the Sneaky Walker had probably never heard of? It might sound ridiculous, but the thought I couldn't get out of my mind was, what if Mr. Douglas heard me, took no offence, and then pretended not to have heard at all? If that was the case, Cobweb the Sneaky Walker wasn't a tattle-tale. And non-tattletales were hard to come by; as Nan would say, they were few and far between. I couldn't help but admire a man like that.

Nan bent down and picked up a round stone, the size of a plum. Closing one eye, she aimed at Oswald Elliot, who was still clinging to one of the elm's thick branches. He yelped louder than the first time.

"Just wanted to make sure you hadn't passed out from dehydration," she called up. "Call it my Christian duty." She patted Cobweb the Sneaky Walker on the arm again. "Leave Tiberius where he is. I think it's a good idea for Oswald to give up his pencils, at least for today. Let him commune with nature, spend some time with the birds. It might give him perspective." Nan turned on her heel, then hesitated. "By the by, Walter, if he comes down before tea time," her voice darkened, "cudgel him."

I lagged behind Nan, distraught. For the first time since the Salem witch trials, there could be a public cudgelling and Nan wasn't going to let me see it. I'd never been to a good cudgelling, not that I wanted Oswald Elliot to be beaten, but there had been something in my Nan's tone, the way she'd glared at him, that made me think it would give her great joy. And there wasn't anything in this life I wanted more than for my Nan to be happy.

I was sure Tiberius was still twitching his tail and licking his chops when we turned into Nan's yard. Tugging on her arm, I pointed back in the direction from which we came. "Nan, do you think Mr. Douglas would like a glass of water? It is rather hot outside, and you asked him to keep watch until tea time."

"He's fine." Nan waved a hand in the air to chase off a troublesome bee. "The man has been in worse places than standing under the shade of an elm tree. A little thirst won't do him in. That one's tougher than nails."

"Well, can I at least hold his cudgel for him? It would be a shame if his arms were too tired to swing it."

CHAPTER 14

AFTER WE LEFT Cobweb the Sneaky Walker under the elm tree, with his mangy cat twitching and waiting for Oswald to fall out of the branches, Nan led me straight to the garden. I followed her with as much dignity as I could muster; I was Anna Karenina with nothing left to live for, and Nan was Countess Vronsky. Countess Vronsky cared little that Anna hated squishing cutworms or pulling weeds. How could she work Anna like a peasant in a garden with no regard for her delicate skin or fainting spells? I wanted to ask, but knew my pleas would fall on deaf ears. In my mind I saw Nan crossing her arms, and with temerity in her voice asking me, *What the hell are you talking about?*

What am I talking about? my Anna would retort, tottering on unsteady legs. *I'm saying I am not made for ruinous labour. My heart isn't capable of such things.* But my hard-hearted Nan would roll her eyes. She'd never see me as Anna Karenina, probably because my Russian was questionable.

Anna Karenina or not, I kept up Griggs' and my deception, never asking who Oswald Elliot was or why Nan so gleefully pelted him with stones, because it might give away what Griggs and I did on the days she minded me. I acted like I only had eyes for Cobweb the Sneaky Walker. Oswald Elliot, for all Nan knew, was someone that didn't quite register in my overactive imagination; I was too busy flapping my fairy wings to bother with Tiberius's catch of the day. Still, I was tempted to raise my hand and suggest Mr. Douglas use my slingshot. It was probably a good idea to soften up the prey before the cudgelling, but I thought better of it. Nan sometimes got after me for my propensity for violence.

I scratched my nose with my pretend gloved hand as I waded into the strawberry patch, careful to step on the stepping stones and not the berries with my Russian rubber boots. Nan bent down to have a go at a patch of weeds.

"He doesn't go to church," I started, a bit unsure as a dispossessed heiress if I should embrace Cobweb the Sneaky Walker. He might be a wolf in sheep's clothing, as Griggs had said.

"Who?"

"Whom," I corrected.

"Who will suffice," Nan said, standing up and rubbing the small of her back.

"Mr. Douglas," I said, just before mouthing Cobweb the Sneaky Walker.

"What does that have to do with the price of rice in China?"

I shrugged. "Griggs says we shouldn't trust him. Can't trust a man that doesn't go to church."

"She does, does she?" Nan pulled the stubborn pigweed she'd eyed earlier.

"Yes ma'am."

"Do you agree with her?"

"I don't know," I said, caught a little off guard. "Griggs is the one who said it. Maybe it's her you should ask."

"I might just do that."

"He only takes his car out on Sundays. And that's not to go

to church; that's to go fishing. Old Lady Griggs says it's a sin. That proves he's shifty."

"Mrs. Griggs says a lot of things." Nan turned her attention to a crooked tomato plant, fastening it to a stake with a bit of string from her sweater pocket. "But not going to church doesn't mean we shouldn't treat him with respect and dignity. And apologize when we've spoken out of turn. Besides, do you think church is the only place God can talk to you?"

I shrugged as I picked a red strawberry. I was about to pop it into my mouth when Nan squatted beside me and took my face between her hands. "Some flowers grow in the sun while others have to be in the shade. I think Mr. Douglas is a shade plant. He can't be expected to be happy in the sun like us."

I looked at Nan and wrinkled my nose. Sometimes she didn't make any sense. "Can you repeat that in Russian?" I asked, taking into consideration the language barrier.

Nan thought a minute and tried again. "God talks to you wherever you listen. And if Mr. Douglas listens best at the lake, that's where God will talk to him. As far as I'm concerned, that man has given more than any one of us can pay back."

I dug the toe of my boot into the dirt and nodded. "I'm still going to call him Cobweb the Sneaky Walker," I said, but not very loud.

CHAPTER 15

NAN WAS WASHING up the lunch dishes when Griggs came wandering up the sidewalk. She was wearing her honeymoon hat, and she yoo-hooed when she glimpsed Nan through the kitchen window. "Oh God," Nan said. "Put the kettle on, Celia, company's afoot."

Old Lady Griggs was through the front door and seated at the table before Nan had her hands dried. "I see you've made yourself at home," Nan said.

Griggs wrinkled her nose. "Why wouldn't I?" She pulled out her hatpin and placed her honeymoon hat on the kitchen table, turning it twice after she set it down.

Nan looked at the hat as she did every time Griggs wore it and set it out as if it were the crown jewels. "It's lovely," she said, with no joy in her voice.

"I know." Griggs rotated it slightly. "I don't know if I told you before, but it was bought for my honeymoon."

"Hence the name," Nan said.

Griggs went on as if Nan had never spoken. "It was sitting in the Happy Valley Druggist's window calling to me. Been there for weeks nestled among the fancy-pants drinking birds and lava lamps, all by its lonesome. The old Mrs. Whitford said it was garish. Can you imagine that? My honeymoon hat *garish*. That woman was cut from the same cloth as her horrific daughter-in-law. She even scolded her son for ordering it, said he should leave the purchases of such merchandise to her." Griggs gave the hat another twist. "I wore it to Danceland, the dance hall at Manitou Beach. They have a spring floor there, hardwood laid over nine inches of horsetail hair."

"You've told me."

"Wilf Carter was singing *There's a Blue Bird on My Windowsill*. Oh, the way that man can warble. Mr. Griggs took my hand in his and twirled me around the dance floor as if I were as light as a feather." Her shoulders shrugged up to her ears. "Wilf winked at me."

"You've told me."

While Nan fussed with the tea and Griggs expounded on the virtues of her honeymoon hat, I slipped under the chrome kitchen table, hoping the handkerchief table cloth would be enough to obscure me from Nan's sightline. It was a perfect spot for spying.

"And then, during the Easter Bazaar last year, Mr. Harkens sat on it. My poor honeymoon hat. I just set it down for a second, and he galumphed over and plopped down like he owned the place. He flattened it and offered me his straw hat as a replacement. I told him you couldn't replace a honeymoon hat Wilf Carter had winked at. Not with something fit for a scarecrow. I had no choice but to punch out the caved in parts and pin my grandma's brooch to the bit that couldn't be salvaged."

"I see."

I saw Nan's legs walk to the table and sit down. She crossed them and rotated her ankle. Nan liked to twist her foot when she was aggravated. I counted the rotations; I think she must have been ready to squash that hat herself.

"How's Celia?" Griggs asked, her voice kind of sticky, like the words were digging into the back of her throat and it was hard to cough them out.

"She's fine. Why do you ask?"

"Oh, I don't know, she looked a little jaundiced the last time I saw her. Likely spending too much time in her room pretending she's Queequeg and hunting dust bunnies."

I could feel my arms get all tingly. I knew the real reason for Griggs' visit. She wanted to know if I'd told Nan about our comic strip adventure, if we had talked about it like me and Archibald did. She was sussing out if I had a tattletale tongue.

I heard a spoon clang against a teacup, and I figured Nan's face was probably as pinched as her voice. "She's not jaundiced, and hunting dust bunnies has yet to be a fatal occupation. As for your concern over her spending too much time in her room, we were in the garden just yesterday, for most of the afternoon in fact."

"Don't take that tone with me, Molly Canterberry. I was just asking out of politeness and for no other reason. My Christian concern for the less fortunate."

"Less fortunate?" Nan sniffed. Griggs was going to get skinned alive. Nan's suspicion was spiking, I knew it was. Griggs was never polite or concerned; usually she was plain obnoxious. It was her strong suit and it was foolish for her to think otherwise; even The Ladies of the Perpetual Indigence Society said so. They wrote it on the top of her Christmas card. Griggs said it was okay to write those kinds of things at Christmas, as long as there was a nice stamp on the envelope for her collection.

To calm my nerves, I started digging out the dirt wedged between the kitchen tiles. That was my downfall. Nan heard me scratching around like a little mouse and she gave me a kick with her hard-soled shoe. I held my breath to keep from crying.

Between Nan's rotating ankle and the pulsating varicose veins on Old Lady Griggs's bony leg, I felt like I'd bitten off more than I could chew. I was in Dante's first circle of hell. The same one Nan said she was in every time she stepped through the door of the Happy Valley Druggist.

The sweat began to trickle down the back of my neck as I looked from Nan's rotating ankle to Griggs throbbing veins; there was going to be a showdown. It was just like the O.K. Corral, when Wyatt Earp and his buddies confronted Billy Claiborne and his gang. I couldn't decide who was who. Was Nan Wyatt Earp or Billy Claiborne? It was hard to say when I only had an ankle and a throbbing vein to examine. I scrunched up smaller, so when Nan kicked Griggs I wouldn't be caught in the crossfire.

Nan turned the screw. "How's the band coming along?" Her ankle slowed to a stop.

"What band?" The vein on Griggs's leg deepened in colour. It was like her very own Pinocchio nose.

"The pot and pan band that you and Celia started."

"Oh that. It's not a real band, the kind that plays at Massey Hall or garden parties." There was a pause. "Hope we didn't get your hopes up."

"Oh, I wasn't hopeful." Nan's ankle resumed rotating.

I could hear Griggs add sugar to her tea cup. She stirred it a little longer than needed. "So, there was a little excitement yesterday."

"Excitement?"

"Yes with Walter Douglas."

Nan drew her foot back, and I was sure she was curling her toes inside her shoe, readying to kick. "Tiberius treed a rat, nothing more."

"If that's the way you want to look at it, but I don't think everyone would agree."

The scrape of tea cups on their saucers was the only sound in the room. I pictured their fingers twitch over their teacup handles as a dust bunny rolled by. I could hardly breathe.

"That man is as mangy as his cat," Old Lady Griggs said after a time.

"Walter?"

"Of course, Walter Douglas. Who else?"

"I've never thought of Walter as mangy, and as for his cat, that poor thing has to be cared for by someone."

"Well that someone needs a bullet and a shovel, I tell you that much."

Nan's ankle twisting doubled in speed. "They need each other. God knows, after Dieppe... And as for Tiberius, that cat has been a godsend. You need to respect that."

"Respect that! I'm tired of respecting anything to do with Walter Douglas. That man needs to take a bath. I can put up with his grunting, scratching, and even," her voice lowered, "his nudity. But not his hygiene. Molly, I can smell him from my kitchen window."

Nan snorted. Old Lady Griggs was the skinniest soul in Happy Valley, and as Nan often said the only thing anyone ever smelled from her kitchen window was her lack of talent.

"And his cat continues to harass the citizens of Happy Valley," Griggs complained. "I feel like a fool, checking to see if that cat is about so I can leave the house to buy groceries. Sometimes he nestles between my doorstep and my begonias, attacking my ankles when I leave the house. I've gone through more nylons than I care to count. And I'm not the only one."

Nan sighed again, and this time Griggs took offence. She banged her spoon on the table. "Don't you dare sigh at me! I'm too old to be sighed at by someone like you."

"And who is someone like me?" Nan's voice was tight, like a plucked guitar string. It was a good question though, one that if

Griggs was wise, she'd take her time to answer. I had to wait and hope for a glimmer of sense.

"Well," Griggs said after a time, "someone who serves me tea in their best china cups."

"These aren't my best cups."

"Potato patato."

Griggs's vegetable talk did nothing to ease the situation; Nan's foot was still rotating, and Griggs's veins were still bulging. I wanted to tap the wiggly worm, send her a message in Morse code, but it was liable to cause a misunderstanding. With Griggs, those were an everyday occurrence. By the time the conversation started up again I'd tamed the dust bunny and she had six little ones of her own.

"Enough of this claptrap," Griggs said. "I'm sure there are more urgent matters to occupy our time."

"Claptrap," Nan repeated. I heard a spoon tap on the table. "I prefer to call it piffle myself."

"Call it what you like, I've come to talk to you about Celia's apology."

Nan stiffened. "What has she done this time?"

I wanted to bite her.

"Nothing. Mr. Griggs told me not to put my oar in, but I can't help myself. As you know, I have Celia's best interests at heart. That being said, I have to let you know, that this time, you've gone too far, Molly Canterberry. Making her apologize to Walter. It must have been humiliating."

I could almost hear Nan's jaw drop. Fur was about to fly. "I beg your pardon?"

"You heard me. Celia needs to know there are some in this community that need to be avoided. In my mind, Walter is at the top of the list."

Nan was silent for a long time, and when she spoke her voice was whispery. "How many coffins were shipped home,

Dorigen? Nine? Ten?" Old Lady Griggs didn't say anything. "Your brother was in one of them. And since then, once a year, we march to the cenotaph, place our hands on our hearts, and promise to never forget. Maybe that's why Walter was the only one who came back. So we don't."

"Don't what?" said Griggs.

"Forget."

I wasn't sure what to do after that. The varicose vein pulsed, but it could have been out of anger, or Griggs may have been thinking about her brother, the one who came home in a box. There was only one thing I could do. Picking up my little dust bunny behind the ears, I ran it ever so gently down her scrawny leg. It didn't have the desired result. Instead of soothing her, it did the opposite. Griggs got up so fast she knocked over the chair and dropped Nan's second-best teacup. It shattered, sending shards across the kitchen floor and under the table.

"If you don't stop your blathering and spitting you'll lose your teeth," Nan said, getting down on all fours to sweep up the broken bits.

"I don't care about my teeth," Griggs shouted as she lifted one corner of the handkerchief tablecloth. "You," she gasped, staring into my wide eyes. "I thought we were past this."

I slipped my dust bunny into my pocket; there was no reason for her to be part of this. "I was trying to soothe you, make your bumpy legs calm down," I said, blinking away the tears.

"If you think I'm going to thank you for putting a fright in me, you have another thing coming."

"Your blood is up," I said, "and you're not thinking clearly."

Griggs jerked upright, knocking the back of her head on the corner of the chrome table. "Celia Canterberry you little scamp, you'll not be telling me when my blood is up or if I'm thinking clearly. I'm of the mind to kick you out of my pot and pan band."

I peeked out from underneath the kitchen table. Even if Nan didn't understand the threat, I did. "Don't do that."

"And why not?"

I didn't know what to say, with Nan standing there, hovering in case I was called something unsavoury. "Because we're friends."

"In a pig's eye."

Nan sighed, handed Griggs her coat, walked over and opened the front door. I didn't even have to apologize for the dust bunny incident.

"Now that's no way for company to behave." I blew out my cheeks and looked up at the clock. "But she made it ten minutes longer than last time."

CHAPTER 16

WITH ALL THE talk about coffins and boys not coming home, I got to thinking about Archibald. She was the best friend a girl could have. She Frankenstein-walked almost as good as me, and all the earthworms on her side of town owed their lives to her. That's why I asked Griggs to deliver an apology note.

"Why would you want me to do that? I've never apologized to your Nan. You can't make a habit of such things."

"But I pulled her hair."

"She deserved it, more than likely, with all her comic strip bragging." Griggs looked me up and down. "I'll do it, but not for the reasons you think. It'll give me a chance to check out their new automatic washing machine. I hear it's a wonder."

She pocketed my note and patted my spot on her plastic-covered chesterfield. I was relieved; I wasn't sure she'd forgiven me for the dust-bunny incident. Griggs never brought it up, and neither did I. We slipped back into our scrapbook explorations without a sideways glance, except now she made sure I was in the line of sight of at least one of her eyes. "Did Oswald Elliot sketch himself high up in that big elm tree this week?" I asked when she pulled the book from under the chesterfield.

She shook her head. "I wish he would have. Hanging on for dear life, while the meanest cat in town licked its chops in anticipation. But I don't think the boy can laugh at himself. Besides, he claims inserting himself into the story goes against his journalistic integrity." She grunted. "Never knew there was such a thing. I think he doesn't dwell in the same reality as the rest of us."

"And what reality is that?"

A look of confusion crossed her face but she didn't answer, instead she changed the subject. "Have I gone over the Poisons and Pixies Halloween Spooktacular? With all this flipping back and forth I've lost track."

I shook my head.

"Didn't think so."

Her fingers twitched as she flipped the scrapbook pages back and forth, her arthritic knuckles oblivious to the speed. She stopped mid-flip and inhaled so deeply I thought her nostrils would stick together. "There," she said, "that's a relief. I knew I had it, hadn't dreamt it this time. The countless hours I spent envisioning these changes before committing them to paper, you'd find it mind-boggling." She slid the scrapbook over, so it was laying partially on my lap. "You must remember this."

My eyebrows shot up. It was a bit of a shock, but I did remember. How could I forget? It had been one of the few times Nan takes me out among the unwashed masses. That is, other than a school day or regular errand run. The colours Griggs had chosen were magical, as if they could coax out someone's secret self with the twist of a crayon.

"I know," Griggs said, examining the embellishments. "It was right after my blue period, when I was delving into a renaissance of colour." Her lazy eye was all dreamy, as if it had joined the ranks of regular eyes, and for just a second got to peer out of the front of Griggs's head. "So much can be expressed by the flick of the wrist, the strength of the grasp, the length of a stroke." She took a deep breath, as if to ground herself. "At times I contribute to the process, and others, like this, I become it. India ink sketches, cartoon alterations, and pencil crayon colouring don't get the respect they deserve. No appreciation. I'm unrecognized in my own time, that's for sure."

She might have a point; Nan never seemed overly thrilled any time I ran out of paper for my doodles and used wall space. But there was no use getting into that now; we were running out of time, and Mr. Griggs wasn't the best at sounding the alarm when Nan came sauntering through the door. Halloween was calling and Griggs, with all her babbling, wasn't listening. I could hardly contain myself; all the sounds and colours were rushing back and knocking on the door of my imagination at the same time. I tapped the black page. "It's just how I remember it," I said, "Except for those extra bits." I pointed to Mrs. Whitford and her braided ear hair. "You might have gotten a little carried away."

"I never get carried away." Griggs straightened and craned her neck. "And if anyone says so, they're no friend of mine."

"Not getting carried away in a bad way," I said, taking back my words in minute spoonfuls. "Getting carried away in ways that inspire others."

Griggs grunted before her neck shrunk down to its regular size. "Thank you for noticing," she said, a little too pleased with herself. "Mr. Griggs is so inspired that most days he doesn't even rise from the kitchen table."

"That's something," I said, and whistled appreciatively.

"I'd say so."

"Nothing like that useless Oswald Elliot! His work is so predictable. He's a bit of a lickspittle, isn't he?"

"If a lickspittle is someone who's an artistic hack, doesn't care about honeymoon hats, and mocks," she looked back towards the kitchen and lowered her voice, "perfectly good husbands for having gout? If that's what it means, I concur."

"I don't think that's what it means."

"Well it should." Griggs dabbed at her ambitious eye with a tissue.

"I know what that's like. When Nan first read me *The Three Musketeers* I was appalled by Cardinal Richelieu."

"Was he a lickspittle too?"

"He was if a lickspittle is a common enemy. If that's true then Richelieu is Oswald Elliot, our adversary, and you're the brave D'Artangnan. That would make Nan Athos and me Porthos."

"D'Artangnan." Griggs rolled the name over her tongue. "I think it suits me."

"Perhaps. He's a bit of a drunk." Griggs didn't say anything. I tapped the back of her hand. "Maybe we can get matching capes."

Griggs lips tightened and the muscles in her cheeks jumped. Someone who didn't know her so well might think I'd said something to irritate her, but I'd spent enough time with her to know almost for certain that she was envisioning the three of us prancing down Happy Valley's main street, in our cavalier boots, swishing our sabres and swearing oaths. The very thought made my fingers prick and the hair stand up on my arms. I checked Griggs's arms; her hairs were laying totally flat, as if they hadn't been eavesdropping on our whole conversation. Idiots.

I turned back to the comic strip page Griggs was studying. "Who's the kid with the pumpkin head?"

"You don't know?"

I shook my head.

"That's you."

"I don't remember dressing up like a pumpkin. I don't even have a pumpkin costume."

I could feel Griggs's body slouch beside mine as if she were a balloon the air had gone out of. "The way Oswald Elliot sees it, your head is seasonal. I thought that was obvious." Griggs looked at me as if I were a simpleton. "As you can see to your left, that's Archibald, she's Little Red Riding Hood. You and your pumpkin head are in the middle and, as you can see, you're the pumpkin-granny."

I touched my head. In all the times Nan and I had gone to the Happy Valley Library, I'd not seen any pumpkin-headed grannies. Not that I had a lot of time to look; the only time Nan let me out of her sight was when she was talking to Miss Libby, the librarian. When the two of them started talking about books there was no stopping them. It was like they lived between the pages and could hardly be pried free. When they were prattling on I slipped into the picture book section, the only section Nan regarded with disdain. She said it treated children as if their brains had oozed out of their ears. For me it was like entering a speakeasy. If Nan caught me she might throw me in the slammer. My spine tingled with excitement.

"Nan's on your right," Griggs said, interrupting my thoughts. "She's in her regular clothes, never been much for dressing up. Not since..." Griggs stopped mid-sentence and ruffled my hair. "Shall I read more?"

"I suppose," I said, still staring at my lopsided Jack-O-Lantern head and my ridiculous green pumpkin stem body, and my pumpkin vine feet. Melon guts spewed from between my carved pumpkin teeth. It wasn't my best look. I had hollow triangle eyes and an indented pumpkin nose. "If I'm supposed to be the granny in that pumpkin getup where's my nightgown and cap? I know I wore them, Nan made them for me out of one of her old bed sheets. She let me push the treadle on her sewing machine myself."

Griggs sniffed. "Huh, I've never noticed that before. To be fair, your head has always been a bit lopsided. It's a commonly held belief that when you were born Nurse Timmer turned a corner too fast, accidentally smashing the good side in. In her defence, newborns are a slippery bunch."

I gave an indignant snort, and Griggs told me if I were going to have hurt feelings about every little thing, it might as well be justified. She tapped the page.

Carnage at the Poisons and Pixies Halloween Spooktacular.

On a beautiful October evening when bright orange pumpkins carved in ghoulish expressions sit amongst the fall leaves, and streamers, dangling skeletons, and ghosts made from old tablecloths hang from the limbs of trees, children with their innocent gazes take it all in, stopping to point at every new marvel that captures their wandering attention, numbing themselves to oblivion with sugary snacks.

Nurse Todd, newly cleared to venture into public again, picks her way through the jubilant crowd, searching for anyone exhibiting aberrant behaviour. "I saw that," *she snaps in a jealous rage as Doc Marley slips his hand a little too low to be around Nurse Timmer's waist.*

Doc Marley, convenient gentleman that he is, draws back. He hooks his cane over his forearm before retrieving a crisp hanky from his inside jacket pocket. Pausing, he presses it to his brow. "I'll have you know, Timmer is my intended."

"Oh, every pretty new young thing is your intended." *Nurse Todd stands on her tiptoes and belts out the words at the top of her voice.* "Put your hands up if Doc Marley has made a similar declaration to you?"

Three frumpy housewives raise their hands.

"See!" Nurse Todd's steely gazed welds itself to Doc Marley's withered face.

Ignoring the housewives, Doc Marley bristles. "I will not be set upon by someone as delusional as yourself."

"Oh, there is no one delusional here, I'm just stating facts. I have eyes to see. Or need I remind you that it was once my slender waist you were groping? Considering you're a man schooled in anatomy, it's surprising how many times your reach fails to find its mark."

Doc Marley's face goes blank.

Rolling her eyes, Nurse Todd turns to the younger woman. "What has he promised you? That he will leave his dead wife? Disown the children he never had? Whisk you away to someplace exotic?"

Nurse Timmer blinks as if she'd lost her moorings, turning this way and that. "Oh my, what to do? What to do?"

Nurse Todd stomps her foot. "Look at me, you foolish simpleton. Don't believe him. The only place he'll send you is Souris Valley, and I can promise you, there is nothing exotic there."

"There is," Doc Marley interjects a little louder than necessary, "if you take your meds."

"I've taken my meds and look where that got me. In the same place I was twenty years ago. Staring at you."

At that the two lovebirds snort, although Nurse Todd's snort is more viscous, as noted by the secretary of The Ladies of the Perpetual Indigence Society. Another reason to deny her membership.

Doc Marley narrows his eyes, forcefully takes his intended's arm, and disappears into the crowd.

Meanwhile, Agnes Obermeyer, in her orange fluffy Halloween slippers, and her dangling lipstick-covered cigarette, has unwisely ambled over and linked arms with Mrs. Whitford, a familiarity that hearkens back to happier times when such an *action would have been readily embraced. But times have changed, and alliances shifted, at least on Mrs. Whitford's part. She tightens her grip on her rhinestone encrusted handbag.* "Have you been drinking, Agnes?"

"Well," Agnes Obermeyer squints, as she lays her head on the other's shoulder, "maybe just a little."

"Just a little? Just a little too much don't you think? Making this crass public display? What will the mayor think? Me hobnobbing with his secretary." *The druggist's wife disentangles herself from the social pariah, thus gaining enough ground to raise her handbag and justifiably beat Mrs. Obermeyer soundly about the head.* "And if I've told you once I've told you a thousand times, you may not be a member of The Ladies of the Perpetual Indigence Society."

Agnes cowers under the onslaught. "I don't have to be an official member," *she cries.* "Just let me straighten the shoes, serve the tea, iron the table cloths."

Mrs. Whitford pauses as if considering the proposition. "No," *she bellows before raising her clutch higher above her hair. When she tries to resume her pummelling, her head lurches forward violently. It seems her pocketbook latch has imbedded itself in her freshly coiffed beehive, undoing her pristinely-crafted appearance. It is conduct very unbecoming of a member of The Ladies of the Perpetual Indigence Society .*

I gasped. Mrs. Whitford looked like Charlton Heston in The Ten Commandments, and I loved that movie. Especially the part when he raised the tablets above his head and then dashed them upon the ground, just like Mrs. Whitford and her handbag. In one frame, her hair was glorious, like spun cotton candy; same as that day in the drugstore before it turned into a tornado full of sticks and baby animals. In the next, thanks to Griggs's handiwork, her eyes were all buggy, and her hair looked like Medusa had crafted her locks out of

Poseidon's petrified entrails. "You don't like Mrs. Whitford, do you?"

"Is it that obvious?"

"Only when you draw on her. To tell you the truth, I long to touch those Medusa locks. Can you imagine doing that and coming away with all your fingers? It would be far more heroic than jabbing Nan with a donkey tail." I smiled at the thought.

"Perhaps, but sadly we'll never know." Griggs was looking as longingly at the snake-haired Medusa head as I was. It was a masterpiece. "That Whitford woman is the self-appointed darling of everything, and the PIS ladies would never let us get close enough to smell her, let alone touch her. That woman would be the babe in the manger at the Happy Valley Christmas Pageant for Wayward Virgins, if she could squeeze her fat arse into the cradle. And it was no different with the Poisons and Pixies Halloween Spooktacular. She strutted around like she was the queen of the pageant." Griggs puffed out her cheeks. "The only thing that brings me comfort is that it's her unexpected hair debacles that bring her any notoriety. It must grate on her; the things she wants forgotten are the only things anyone remembers." With glee Griggs resumed her reading.

Mrs. Obermeyer curls in a ball at the other's feet, whimpering and pulling at Mrs. Whitford's knee-high nylon stockings. "Is this any way to treat your sister, your one and only sibling?"

With a final tug, Mrs. Whitford fails to dislodge the clasp, leaving her clutch swinging helplessly from her sunken beehive. The leader of The Ladies of the Perpetual Indigence Society is forced to pelt her simpering sibling with whatever treats she can grab from the baskets of passersby. She reduces several small children to tears, but their parents are too wary to do anything about it. "I told you not to call me that anymore," Mrs. Whitford roars. "Any blood we had in common died when *we buried our unfortunate parents. We are now and forever unconnected."*

My eyes widened. When Griggs had started reading, she'd described a Happy Valley that was beautiful, with children wandering in a Halloween wonderland. But within every cartoon frame there was only strife and ruin. "Where's the numb oblivion?"

Griggs grunted. "Well, in this town that's as numb as it gets. I suppose it might look like mayhem to an outsider, but when you've lived here all your life, you should know numb when you see it. As peaceful gatherings go, what you see here is as close to a Hallmark Card as Happy Valley gets. A little bit of harmless banter, some playful taunting, and a light clobbering; it's been like that for years. Until you showed up. That's when things started to go awry." She shook her head and clicked her tongue.

"Can we get back to Mrs. Whitford pelting her sister with Halloween candy?"

After a bit of grumbling Griggs cleared her throat. Soon we were back at the Poisons and Pixies Halloween Spooktacular where my pumpkin-headed doppelgänger galumphed around eating worms and pulling legs off spiders. All the other cartoon people, except the ones Griggs altered, had normal heads, and they moved out of my pumpkin-head way, stepping around the seeds and pumpkin guts dripping from my serrated mouth. Nurse Timmer fainted when I thumped by, falling into Doc Marley's waiting arms, his old-man frame crumpled under her young-woman weight.

The other cartoon children were dressed in all kinds of costumes — witches, scarecrows, ghouls and skeletons — and lined up for apple bobbing. Me and Archibald waited our turns. Archibald, in her Little Red Riding Hood outfit, was swinging her basket as if it were a weapon while Nan hovered over my shoulder like she was waiting for some giant vulture to swoop down and peck out my eyes. There wasn't anyone at the Poisons and Pixies Halloween Spooktacular willing to take us on. Griggs, to her credit, had coloured each frame with such care, it was as if she hoped it might hang in the Louvre one day.

"It's a work of art, I know," Griggs said, admiring her handywork.

"What are all the splotchy bits?"

"Oh those. Kind of looks like a bunch of bugs hitting a windshield doesn't it?"

I nodded.

"That's blood."

"I don't remember there being any blood."

"Neither do I."

The only thing I remembered was Mrs. Billboson cutting in line with Billy. He turned to me and Archibald and stuck out his fat tongue. Archibald thumped him with her basket and I plucked out Larry, Moe and Curly one at a time. "I didn't know hair could bleed."

"It doesn't, but that won't make a very good strip. Sadly, your Nan pulled you off before you went for his eyebrows." She placed a black ribbon between the pages and closed the book. "I think it should have been called the *Carnage in the Bobbing-For-Apples Line*. More to the point. People are still talking about it, and most believe what Oswald depicted, rather than what they saw. It's more horrifying that way."

I didn't know what to think. The way Oswald Elliot drew me, it was no wonder Nan was too tired to go out most nights. It was like she was carting around her own little grim reaper with tiny scythe hands. My pencil-drawing-self limped across the page huffing and drooling, without a backward glance to the misery left in my wake.

I could feel my throat get tight around my breath. According to Griggs, almost everyone in Happy Valley thought my birth was the start of the town's demise. I tucked my knees closer to my chest, making myself as small as I could, bit my lip, and blinked away my tears.

"What about Tommy Harken's uncle?" I asked. "He came back from the war with one leg and a bottle of paper-bag whiskey. That's not my fault, I wasn't even born yet."

"That may well be, but there are those who would disagree. They'd call it foreshadowing. For instance, take Tiberius, he was just a wide-eyed kitten the day you came into the world, and now he's a menace to society. Coincidence?" Griggs raised an eyebrow. "Some don't think so. And as for Tommy Harken's uncle, after he came out of his coma, he spent most of his days laying on his couch taking swigs and using the Lord's name in vain. He never did that before you were born."

"Maybe it's because of the war. Nan said it changed Mr. Douglas."

"Your Nan says a lot of things, but that's not what The Ladies of the Perpetual Indigence Society think."

I hugged my legs harder and looked back down at the strip. This wasn't going the way I'd hoped. Sketches of my should-have-been ma with her warty skin didn't bother me so much. As Griggs would say, her behaviour was unbecoming to anyone who considered themselves a homogeneous homo sapien. So, I figured my should-have-been got what she had coming. But when it happened to me, it felt different. When I was the one all distorted and frothing at the mouth, there was no joy in it.

If this was all there was to my past, maybe the PIS ladies were right. "Perhaps you missed something," I said, flipping at the edge of the pages with a fingertip.

"Miss something!" Griggs slapped my hand away. "What kind of fool do you take me for?"

"I didn't know there were different kinds."

Griggs flinched. "Of course there aren't different kinds.

Sometimes you say the strangest things. I've spent the better part of the morning orating your young life and I swear, you haven't appreciated a minute of it, not a bit. My throat is parched from my excellent vocalizations, my eyes strained from looking through these filthy spectacles. And don't get me started on the emotional toll." She stifled a sob before ripping the glasses from her face.

"Why don't you clean them?"

"That's Mr. Griggs' job." She lowered her voice. "And he's not been himself lately. It's like the cat's got his tongue."

"Tiberius?"

"No! Don't you take anything seriously? It was a — what does your Nan call it? A witticism."

I didn't think Griggs was right. That's not what Nan would call it, but who was I to argue?

CHAPTER 17

THE NEXT TIME I saw Griggs she was in her kitchen ironing her husband a fresh plaid shirt. "We're not reading the scrapbook today," she said.

"Why not?" I was rather disappointed. When Nan had been washing up the breakfast dishes, I had hand-lotioned the backs of my legs to prepare for her sticky, plastic-covered chesterfield.

She set the iron down. "I've only asked one thing of you, Celia Canterberry. One thing. From the day you were born to this one, mention my honeymoon hat in public."

"I did."

Old Lady Griggs spit on the iron and resumed her task. "And why have I not heard of it, pray tell?"

I shrugged. "Maybe Oswald Elliot didn't hear me. I'm sure he was lurking in the grocery store aisles. Thought I caught a glimpse of his plaid pants through the canned peas."

"That's ridiculous. With ears that size, nothing could get past the boy."

"Well, your honeymoon hat did. As for me, that hat has caused nothing but trouble." That got me thinking. If anyone knew about what Nan didn't want me to know, it was Griggs. She was always sticking her bony nose where it didn't belong. "When Nan was a bride," I said, as carefree as I could, "who bought *her* honeymoon hat?"

Griggs face went white, and without even thinking, she set the iron, flat on its tummy, in the middle of her husband's plaid shirt. It wasn't long before smoke billowed around its edges, steaming like it was ready to catch fire. "There are some things I don't have it in me to recall," Griggs said when she finally lifted the iron, not seeming to care about the blackened triangle it left behind. She leaned over and brushed the hair out of my eyes. "The laundry can wait, let's mosey into the living room. There are some strips I've been meaning to show you."

"I thought you said we weren't going to look at the scrapbook today."

"Do you believe everything I say?"

"No."

"Then why ask stupid questions?" Griggs plopped down on the plastic-covered chesterfield and I slithered up beside her, my lotioned legs like butter in a hot frying pan. She tapped a finger on the scrapbook cover. "You know, Celia, when I started showing you my creations, I had no idea I'd enjoy your company. Was only watching you as a favour. Over the years your Nan has done so much for me. She helped me with Mr. Griggs's eyes, held his head while I sewed them on. No one else would've done that for me. I want you to remember that."

"Now that you've told me, how could I forget? It's horrifying."

"It was quite an evening. Oh, how we laughed." Griggs's lazy eye bobbed up and down as if it were reliving the whole thing.

"Did you sew on any other body parts?"

"Of course not. We're not barbarians." She flipped open the scrapbook. "Have I shown you your first Easter?"

I shook my head.

"Well I suppose it wasn't your first, but it was the first time you came out to the Happy Valley Easter Eggstacular. And I must say, you were something! Gathering eggs ambidextrously, while others bumbled around like they were in the dark. Your Nan was so proud, until —" Griggs paused, "but I'm getting ahead of myself."

I scanned the strip as Griggs did her vocal exercises. This time I didn't have to ask her which one was me. I was unmistakable, there in the centre of the frame, a child with a humpty-dumpty head teetering on china-doll ankles; my feet had already crumbled away. Griggs had coloured me like a fabulous Fabergé egg, and I had never looked so elegant, with fancy swirls and viney blooms. I leaned over and smelled me.

"Your Nan sewed you the cutest outfit, made it from her favourite Sunday dress, a tear with every stitch. I think she knew she'd never wear anything that fine again. And all Oswald shows of it is a row of Battenberg lace tight around your egg neck, separating your head from your porcelain legs." Griggs licked her lips and began to read:

It Has Risen. On a bright Easter Sunday, hope hangs in the air. Children skip through dew-soaked grass while woodland creatures frolic in the shadows of the budding elms. Nestled in amongst the verging dandelions and spring violets, Easter eggs wait to be discovered.

Standing on her tiptoes, Mrs. Whitford scans the crowd. "They're not here," she says to her husband, referring to The Ladies of the Perpetual Indigence Society. "It's hardly worth our time staying."

Mr. Whitford shifts from one foot to the other. "They could be on their way. Let's give them more time."

"I don't think so. We'll leave and come back later, can't make an entrance when there is no one of importance to watch." The Whitfords climb back into their shiny new automobile and begin circling the block.

Meanwhile, Doc Marley sets up a table next to Happy Valley's only ambulance, kindly volunteering to provide on-the-spot medical evaluations. Across the way, Frank Murray trots out the latest fashions from the 'up and coming' collection at his haberdashery, while Farmer Hempel putters in on his old Massey Ferguson tractor, in hopes he might coerce Mayor Forde into having Happy Valley's first tractor pull.

Wandering into all the frivolity is Molly Canterberry and the child of ill-gotten-means. The two enter the mix with not so much as a by your leave to examine the bake table. Miss Canterberry comments on the strawberry rhubarb pie that Agnes Obermeyer insists is fresh, whilst anyone in their right mind knows both strawberries and rhubarb are out of season.

"Fresh out of my deepfreeze," Agnes cackles, her crinkled cigarette bobbing up and down, stuck to her lipstick.

"You should have said that in the first place," Miss Canterberry replies. "Mrs. Billboson might have not lodged a complaint with the judges."

"I'll give her something to complain about." Agnes slips off one of her pink and blue fuzzy bedroom slippers and wings it at the complainer's head. "That'll teach you," she bellows, "think you're so high and mighty."

Drawn to the dazzling Ford Fairlane, the youngest Canterberry slips from her guardian's grasp and darts in front of the unsuspecting Mrs. Whitford, who, unable to see the egg-like obstacle careening towards her due to her motherly expansion, tries to hoist her ample girth out of her automobile. "Get over here," she says through gritted teeth to her loving husband, "and free me from this contraption."

Mr. Whitford looks weary. "Can't we use the hoist at the garage, or Mr. Hempel's tractor? He wanted a pull."

"I'll give you a pull, and believe me you won't like it."

Grasping his wife's underarms and bracing his feet in the frame of the car door, Mr. Whitford heroically frees his better half.

"If my dress is wrinkled, I'll never forgive you," the Mrs. says by way of thanks.

"I don't think you have to worry," Mr. Whitford replies, examining the frock. "I'm going to have to use the Jaws of Life just to rescue the thing."

Mrs. Whitford doesn't respond, but the withering look she gives her husband would have left a lesser man scampering for the shelter of his automobile. Not Mr. Whitford. He struts towards the Ford Fairlane as if he doesn't have a care in the world. But he's barely slammed and locked the door when tragedy strikes. The eggheaded Canterberry child tangles herself up in Mrs. Whitford's trunk-like legs.

One minute Mrs. Whitford is stepping gingerly onto the lush green grass, calling, "Yoo-hoo, we have arrived," to The Ladies of the Perpetual Indigence Society. The next, Molly Canterberry's granddaughter totters into her path, upending the undelivered mother. The humpty-dumpty head gets to her feet, shakes herself off, and continues on her way, oblivious to the carnage she has caused.

Mrs. Whitford, poor Mrs. Whitford, remains where she is, heaving and wailing. She calls out to her husband, "Get her! The wretch has attacked me."

The Ladies of the Perpetual Indigence Society rush forward en masse, passing their prostrate companion to confront the stunned Miss Molly Canterberry.

"We told you not to bring her! We begged you to keep her locked up and now look what she's done." The group parts to reveal Mrs. Whitford being taken away on a stretcher, as the egg-child collects small look-a-likes from among the spring dandelions.

"She's in labour," Nurse Todd announces, as she runs beside the stretcher. "Where's Doc Marley?"

"Where he always is after observing lent. He's giving free medicals inside the ambulance." With a heave, Ned, the part-time ambulance driver, full-time barstool warmer, has foolishly taken one of the stretcher poles. Three others grab hold of the remaining poles, though none resemble Mr. Whitford.

Nurse Todd grows pale. "He promised."

Ignoring the nurse's quivering bottom lip, the men each redden in the face and almost buckle under their load. "What have they been feeding her?" Ned's voice is strained by the effort.

Mrs. Whitford shifts on the stretcher. "What do they feed me?" she shrieks, her voice shrill. "I'll have you know I'm eating for two."

"Well," Ned says, "it feels like we're carrying for four."

Upon reaching the ambulance, the stretcher is roughly set down and Ned flings open the ambulance door. "Doc Marley," he says as the door swings wide, "we brought you a customer."

"I already have one," Doc Marley replies, wiping his mouth with the back of his hand, a smear of lipstick left in its wake.

"My wife?" Ned bellows. "Your customer is my wife?"

"And a grateful wife she is." Doc Marley winks at Ned's wife as she juts her chin high in the air and steps out of the ambulance. Her blouse is only partially buttoned.

Balling his hands into fists, Ned's lips twitch. "If you weren't the only doctor in the county and she didn't need you," he indicates to the wailing Mrs. Whitford, "we'd have more than a talk about this."

"Good thing I'm needed then." Doc Marley steps aside as the

men slide the stretcher into the ambulance. He takes Mrs. Whitford by the wrist and looks at his watch.

Taking the keys from his pocket, Ned climbs into the front seat of the ambulance, swearing as he does so. Nurse Todd clambers into the passenger's side. "I can't believe that man."

"I can't believe my wife. She's not even ill." He lifts one hand from the steering wheel and pounds the dash. No matter how loudly he protests, he is out-done by Mrs. Whitford's labour pains. Careening into the hospital parking lot, Ned doesn't even touch the brakes; a power pole brings the ambulance to an abrupt halt. "Who put that there?"

Nurse Todd lifts her face from the dash. "The same people that built the hospital."

"Well it's not there anymore."

The pole that had proudly stood by the medical centre for nigh forty years, had cracked, tipped over and broken through the hospital roof, coming to rest in the storage room.

"Isn't that the room where Morris keeps his still?"

"Use to be? Now it seems to be the origin of the fire." Ned and Nurse Todd sit in the ambulance and watch the flames lick their way from one window to the next. "Do you want to help Doc Marley in the back?" Ned asks.

Nurse Todd leans back in her seat and listens to Mrs. Whitford's vocalizations. "No, he sounds like he's doing fine all on his own."

Griggs closed the scrapbook. "That's why the Whitfords have a wing of the hospital named after them. If she hadn't gone into labour early, we would still be using that drafty old building."

I thought about all the sick patients limping to escape the inferno. Ned and Nurse Todd had been watching it like it was some kind of wiener roast.

"The hospital was empty," Griggs assured me, noticing my

concern. "Most were released so they could attend the Happy Valley Eggstacular. The others had gone home just to avoid the food."

"Is there a wing named after me?"

"Not at the hospital; yours is at the prison." Griggs tilted her head. "And that's no mean feat, you're the only one under the age of ten who's been given such an honour. Not even Archibald. *The Little Miss Canterberry Wing for Unredeemable Wretches*. You should be proud." She paused to clarify. "Canterberry proud, not Griggs proud. Canterberry proud is a whole other playing field."

"Do you have a wing named after you?"

"What a question. Do you think either I or Mr. Griggs would have ever, ever behaved in a notorious manner?" She didn't wait for a response. "We are church-going people who pride ourselves on our eccentricities, but never have we stepped a hairy toe over the line to barbarity."

"Neither have I. And my toes aren't hairy."

"Not according to Oswald Elliot. In this strip alone, you were the cause of the tragedy at the old Happy Valley Hospital."

I couldn't argue with her there; the hospital had burnt but I thought it was more from poor driving than anything else. "What about Nan? Has she ever had a building named after her?"

"No, why would she?"

I shrugged. "How about her man?"

"What man?"

"The one who gave her a honeymoon hat."

Griggs snorted, and she spoke in choppy, tight words. "No one has given your Nan such a hat. And I think it's best if you don't ask about it again."

"Did he die in the war?" I thought he must have been a

brave hero or a stealthy spy that slipped in and out of enemy lines. Nan wouldn't have had any other. "Is it too painful to talk about?"

Griggs went quiet for a long time, looking at her nails, shifting her weight from one bony cheek to the other on her plastic-covered chesterfield. Her skin was the colour of death, as if we were tiptoeing on evil's edge. "Why can't you let well enough alone? You'll have to ask your Nan about that." Her lips twisted as she slipped the book back under the chesterfield. "I think it's best you go home now."

"But Nan said you were to watch me."

"Are you planning on doing anything bad?"

"No."

"Then what's to watch?"

CHAPTER 18

I WALKED to Nan's house as slowly as I could, stopping every so often to look back. I thought Griggs might regret her decision and wave me in, but there was no waving. Griggs stood behind her lace curtains, shaking her head. I couldn't figure out what I had done wrong. I hadn't touched things that weren't mine, made light of any of her strange ways, or her lazy eye. The only thing I'd done was ask about a honeymoon hat, and it seemed to have changed everything.

It seemed like just yesterday we had toasted each other with orange Freshie in Tupperware glasses, laid out her best pots and pans for our band, and made fun of Mrs. Whitford and her lopsided beehive hairdo. We couldn't get any closer than that. I even got to eat off her best honeymoon china. A plate that had been re-glued when Mr. Griggs hadn't reached out his cotton-stuffed hand to receive it. I sat on her furniture and was never accused of having head lice or any of the other ailments the PIS ladies claimed I had. And now I was cast out because I had asked a simple question? None of it made sense.

I was still puzzling things out when I rounded the hedge that skirted Nan's yard. I gasped and my lotioned legs froze solid. There in my Nan's driveway was that sputtering, rusty, old grey truck. My should-have-been pa's truck. It was just like at the hospital, except no one was yelling out its window or taking swigs out of brown bottles. It was all I could do not to run back and tell Griggs. She'd be in her glory, stumbling upon a scene that she'd only dreamt of. I could picture her scratching her bony bottom as she licked her lips, preparing for Oswald Elliot's signature profile sketch. That would be something, her lazy eye working double quick, scanning this way and that, while her ambitious eye helped me catch the intruders red-handed. Oswald would have had a field day. His pencil would hardly be able to capture the wonder of us.

The only thing that stopped me from turning tail was that Griggs would need time to poke out the dents in her honeymoon hat and scavenge her lumpy orange lipstick from the bottom of her straw handbag. It would give my should-have-beens a chance to escape, and I couldn't have that.

I dropped to my belly and snake-slithered to the truck, stood, opened the door, and slid onto the front seat. I could smell my should-have-been pa all sweaty and beer soaked. I closed my eyes and thought of how Oswald had drawn him. All haggard and chapped, his hands cracked from dryness. He might be a better man if they were silky smooth. Maybe a banker or rodeo clown. He wouldn't have to be a should-have-been any more. Nan's cold cream would do the trick. I didn't have any cold cream, so I did the next best thing; I looked for the nearest mud puddle, and wrapped the steering wheel in earth worms. I could imagine my should-have-been's surprise. "My thieving hands are so supple now," my should-have-been pa would say. "Might as well take up banking."

The idea made me warm inside, that Nan would be so proud of me for showing kindness to the derelicts who'd abandoned me. It was the little things that make life worth living.

I slithered through the green grass and blooming dandelions and plastered myself to the side of the house. Nan had left the kitchen window open, hoping to catch a breeze. Luckily for me, the opening let out just enough sound so I could eavesdrop on my should-have-beens. They seemed to be bickering with one another, the way Griggs did with her husband. He was always giving her the silent treatment.

Standing beneath the window I stilled my heart. It was the first time I heard my should-have-been's voices. They weren't at all like I'd thought; there was no kindness in them, and not a bit of regret.

"Are you ready?" my should-have-been pa called from the kitchen. I could hear him opening and closing cupboard doors.

"Hold your horses, we just got here," my should-have-been ma snapped back.

"You said you'd be quick."

"How was I supposed to know the old cow was going to switch up her hiding places?"

"She's your old cow."

"Doesn't mean I can read her mind. All you need to do is put things back the way you found them."

"I know the drill."

My eyes went wide; she'd called Nan an old cow. Old Lady Griggs didn't even do that. I scrunched up my face and regretted wrapping the steering wheel with those supple earthworms.

There was more shouting back and forth and my should-have-been pa's voice walked out of earshot. The whole thing made me want to pee. The should-have-beens were in Nan's house unattended, and the screen door hadn't been latched and was banging in the breeze. It was enough to get my ire up. I slithered across the side of the house, picking my way around the spring daffodils and Nan's dud tulip bulbs, the ones she'd gotten from The Ladies of the Perpetual Indigence Society's annual fundraiser. Nan said she should have known better; anything connected with that outfit was bound to disappoint.

When I had passed the last tulip and was inching around the peonies that ants seemed overly fond of, I heard voices again. They were belching through the screen door. I moved onto the front step and pushed the screen door shut, my face against the mesh. The should-have-beens were nowhere in sight, but I could hear them rifling through Nan's things.

"Hello," I whispered to the air. Not so much as a flutter of a response. My fingers found a tiny rip in the screen, and began to pick at it. Before I knew it, my whole hand was through the opening. A little larger and I could slip my head through. And when Nan got mad at the ruined mesh, I'd tell her it must have been Tiberius after her fresh butter. It had happened before.

Once my body was through, I looked back at the hole I'd made. It was a bit big for a cat, and I wondered if Nan would notice. There was a bang, and I turned towards the sound. It had come from upstairs, Nan's bedroom. With as much stealth as I could I dropped on all fours. I didn't slither this time, I scampered. Scampered at such a speed my should-have-beens would have been hard pressed to see me. I was up the stairs and outside Nan's door before I could say Jack Robinson.

That's when out of the corner of my eye I spotted her. She hadn't noticed me, she was too busy sifting through Nan's underwear drawer. And not her everyday one either. She was going through the one Nan saved for special occasions. The one with all her scarfs and pantyhose that weren't all soaped up to stop a run. Nan hardly ever opened that drawer. My heart flip-flopped. My should-have-been ma had her head wrapped with a peacock scarf that Griggs had brought back from the big city. Tufts of my should-have-been ma's caramel hair stuck out from its silk edges. I couldn't help staring at the scarf. Nan had been saving it for a grand entrance.

My should-have-been-ma looked up from what she was doing and saw my reflection in the mirror. "So you're the girl," she said, as if she were talking to a dead fly. She kept shuffling through Nan's dainties.

I didn't say anything.

Slamming shut Nan's underwear drawer, she turned and scanned the room. I didn't think there was a corner she hadn't dug into with her grimy fingers. "Be a dear and tell me where your grandma's best hiding places are." My should-have-been-ma gave me a smile that dripped with honey, but her eyes were all pinpricky.

That honey look made me want to tell her, it even made me want to like her. But her pinpricky eyes made me want to crawl under my bed.

"Where are they?" she said stepping closer.

"She has lots of hiding places," I said, wanting her to think Nan had shown me all her hidey-holes. That we were as close as any other throw-away granddaughter and didn't-want-any-help gran. It was the wrong thing to say. My should-have-been-pa must have heard me from wherever he was. He came barreling up the stairs and grabbed me by the shoulders.

"So, this is the mouse, the one scurrying around, avoiding the traps."

I swallowed hard. "What traps?"

"That's for me to know and you to find out. I just have one question for you. Where? Where are her hiding places?" He squeezed me so tight I thought my arms would pop right off. I tried to pull away, but he squeezed harder, and gave me a little shake. "I asked you a question, you little freak."

I looked into my should-have-been-pa's face for the first time, and had difficulty catching my breath. He had butter-yellow teeth; never saw that in the comic book strip. I wondered if mice tried to lick them when he was sleeping, leaving buttery paw prints where they walked. His teeth were even worse than my should-have-been ma's pinprick eyes. He shook me again and I tried to think but my should-have-been ma moved in right beside him, her eyes as tight on me as his squeezing hands.

My should-have-been pa leaned in a little closer. "Well open that smug little mouth of yours and spill it."

"I broke the cookie jar," I said, a little trembly. "That was a regular spot. And I set fire to her everyday kitchen table flower arrangement when trying to light a nub of a candle. Nan used to stuff her extra pocket money under the wax apple, the one beside the chipped wax pear, even though whenever Old Lady Griggs came over for tea she tried to pluck a piece of fruit from the basket and chomp down on it. Nan said it was most likely a godsend, me setting the thing on fire; sooner or later someone would have sussed out her hiding spot. Then there was the time I nailed down the jiggling floor board. Nan said she'd used up that stash the day before, so it didn't matter."

My should-have-been pa clapped one hand over my mouth. "I didn't ask for your life history. I don't care, never have, never will." His lips twitched. "Where is the stash now?"

I didn't know. After I plundered all her old hiding places, Nan kept her new ones to herself. But I didn't think the should-have-beens would believe me if I told them that. The only place I could think of showing them was my own hiding place. The place where I kept my birthday money. They followed me down the hall and into my bedroom, jabbing me between the shoulder blades whenever I hesitated. I walked past my sailboat bed, and nodded at Captain Ahab; he was a late riser, still screwing on his peg leg. Dropping to my knees I pulled up the floor grate. "It's down there," I said, moving the dust bunny that was guarding it. "Here." I handed them a small tin box.

My should-have-been ma hooked her chin over my should-have-been-pa's shoulder. "What do we have here?" she said as he pried open the dented lid. "The treasures of a freak."

My should-have-been-pa plucked out my four silver dollars from between the buttons, cat's eye marbles, and rubber balls. He had the same disappointed look on his face as Mrs. Whitford had when I gave her daughter a haircut. What did they expect from a seven-year-old?

"Is this all there is?"

"Yes sir."

"You're not lying are you?"

I shook my head. My dust bunny growled.

"The little scamp." My should-have-been-ma leaned over and pinched my cheek, twisting it before she let it go. "She doesn't know any of the old bat's hiding places any more than I do." Her eyes pricked. "And I thought it would be different this time."

I blinked away my tears.

"The more things change, the more they stay the same." My should-have-been pa flicked me in the head. "And don't be running to your grandmother about this, cause we'll be watching."

I shook my head and crossed my heart.

"We'll come back if you do," my should-have-been pa warned, his butter teeth disappearing behind tight lips. "And you won't like it."

The screen door banged and Tiberius's unnatural yowl stilled the air. "How the hell did they know we'd be here?" my should-have-been pa spat.

My should-have-been ma put her snarling face close to his. "Well, they didn't hear it from me."

I thought there was going to be a long-awaited cudgelling, and went to grab Captain Ahab's spare peg leg, but once again the should-have-beens were a disappointment. There wasn't even a mild dustup. The two of them rushed to my bedroom window, slid it up, and as quick as you like, shimmied down the drain pipe, as if they had done it a thousand times before.

The last thing I heard my should-have-been pa say was, "Who the hell wrapped goddamned earthworms around my goddamned steering wheel?"

From my window I watched the rusty grey truck spit up gravel as it sped out of Nan's drive, Nan's peacock scarf still wrapped around my should-have-been ma's greasy head. My should-have-beens didn't even turn to wave. When they were out of sight, I ran downstairs so fast that when I rounded the corner to the kitchen, I was almost bowled over by Cobweb Sneaky Walker and Tiberius. The three of us eyed each other before Cobweb nodded and I climbed on the stool Nan kept under the wall telephone and dialed the operator. "Get me Oswald Elliot at the Happy Valley Journal," I said, reaching up and taking hold of one of Cobweb Sneaky Walker's trembling hands.

CHAPTER 19

THE NEXT TIME I saw the cartoon strip it wasn't on Griggs's plastic-covered chesterfield. Our pot and pan band wasn't strewn across the living room floor. Mr. Griggs wasn't keeping guard in the kitchen, ready to spring on anyone who passed by. It was just me and Nan. In Nan's kitchen at Nan's breakfast table. She came into the room, her hands shaking, and dropped the newspaper with a thud. "Celia?" she said. "Is this true?"

I looked up from my cereal bowl and shrugged. I didn't know what else to do, Nan had never allowed a newspaper into the house before, and I had to stop myself from being overly excited; the way Griggs and I were when we scanned the pages. I licked out my cereal bowl to stop my fingers from twitching. I was torn between pretending I'd never seen a newspaper before and ripping through it to see how Oswald Elliot had drawn me, and what kind of head I had this week.

Nan lifted my chin with the tip of a finger, and I let my face go slack. She was looking for something and I prayed she didn't find it. With a grunt, Nan finished her search and flipped open the paper, tapping the first frame with all of her impatience. "Celia, is this true?"

My eyes glanced to where Nan was pointing. My heart fell, not because of the story the pictures told, I hadn't had a good look at them yet, but because of Oswald's drawing. I wanted to tell Nan about Griggs's embellishments, her bright colours, her India ink curlicues. In comparison, Oswald Elliot was rather useless, there was no chiaroscuro. "Well, it's nothing to write home about."

Nan tapped the page again. "Celia, you need to answer me. Were those people here? In this house? In my house?"

I nodded.

Her voice caught. "Why didn't you tell me?"

"They told me not to. Said they'd come back. That's when Cobweb Sneaky Walker came and chased them away."

"Thank God." Nan blinked away tears. "But what about them?" She jabbed the strip before she gave me a quick scan. "What did they do? Did they touch you, hurt you?"

I shook my head, a little crestfallen. "Not really. I kind of wish they had, then Oswald Elliot could have drawn them with stripes and manacles, clinking down the hallways of the Happy Valley Penitentiary, yelling over the fence at the children on the playground." I could feel myself start to whine; I couldn't help it. "How could he miss the butter teeth and pinprick eyes? I told him all about it; I could have scratched my initials in that softness. And he drew my should-have-been ma and pa hunchbacked and gnarled, looking like midnight droolers waiting to pop out someone's marmalade eyes to spread on their toast. The same ones who probably carved in my headboard with your best butter knife. They weren't midnight droolers. Droolers disappear in the light of day. Everyone knows that. My should-have-beens didn't wither in the sun."

I stopped when I was sure Nan was still impressed, leaving out the bit about her peacock scarf she was saving for a special occasion. I craned my neck to look at the strip: I was crisp and spotless, a regular Christmas tree angel topper. Without an Easter egg head or jagged pumpkin mouth, it took me a minute to recognize myself as a normal-looking kid. It was kind of disappointing. It took the wind out of my sails. How could I get all offended when the kid in the panel looked as lovely as all the Dionne quintuplets rolled up into one?

"All of that on your first perusal?" Nan interrupted my musing.

I nodded.

"Quite an art aficionado." Nan stiffened beside me. "I have a few questions for you. First of all, how do you know Oswald Elliot?'

"Miss Dobbs talked about him in first grade art class. She said some of us could be Rembrandts, while others with facial abnormalities, like Shelly Shepard, could be van Goghs. And finally there were those who insist on dog-paddling in the shallow end of the gene pool, like any one of the Obermeyer clan; they could be Oswald Elliots. I think she used to be sweet on him; Archibald says she saw them parked behind the curling rink. The windows of the car were all steamed up, so they were hard to make out. But she knew it was them because it was Miss Dobbs' car, and Oswald Elliot's banana-seat bike was sticking out of the open trunk. Now Miss Dobbs calls him a three-minute egg, but I think she still smells like pee, and that would chase off any man."

Nan started fanning herself. "Where do you hear such things?"

I shrugged. "I've got more."

"God, I hope not." Nan ran a hand through her hair. "Celia," she said, taking both my hands in hers, "I need you to focus. Do you think you can do that?"

"I think so."

"Good. The intruders, why would you think they were your parents? Your should-have-beens?"

"That's tricky," I said, buying time. "I was wondering the same thing myself."

"Well?"

"Photosynthesis," I said in a spooky voice.

Nan wasn't impressed. "You mean osmosis."

"Same difference."

"Not really."

I changed the subject, hoping to throw her off her game. "Oswald Elliott drew your house all wrong. The outside is right; the outside is all peeling paint and crooked shutters, anyone that walks by can see that. But the insides, he didn't even make a good guess. The ceilings are too high, and there aren't any stockings hanging from chandeliers." I wanted to tell her Griggs could fix things, add bubbles to the bathtub Oswald had filled with gin and show the furniture as it really was, a little beat up but not being whittled away by termites. "It's a rookie mistake," I said generously. "We should have him over for tea."

"We will do no such thing."

"If we don't educate him, no one will, and then how is he supposed to win the Pulitzer Surprise?"

"Oh, my God!" Nan slumped into a chair and was quiet for a long time. Her breathing was fast at first, but then she started counting and it slowed. "We can deal with Oswald Elliot later," she finally said. "Right now I need you to focus, remember?"

I nodded.

"What happened?"

"The man squeezed my shoulders and the woman glared at me with pinpricky eyes."

"What did you do?"

"Wrapped their steering wheel with earthworms."

She smiled and her hand brushed my cheek. "Why am I not surprised?"

Nan took a deep breath and the questions started again. She wanted to know why I hadn't told her, and was I scared, and if I could ever bear to be alone again. I said they made me promise not to, and I was only scared late at night, when the moon shone on the jaggity writing on my headboard, and I liked being alone, except when she wasn't there. Nan seemed pleased with my answers, but she had one last question.

Nan slid her chair closer. "How did Oswald find out about the break-in?"

"I phoned him."

"Phoned him?" She rubbed her forehead, and her lips twisted back and forth, as if she were mulling over her thoughts and didn't like how they tasted. With a little more mulling and chewing, she pulled me on to her lap and kissed me on the top of the head. "I'm so sorry," she said, her head laid on top of mine. "I'm so very sorry."

I wanted to tell her there was no need to apologize, but I liked being close like that. And if I spoke, I was scared she might think of some chores that needed to be done, or check to see if I remembered to wash behind my ears. (I hadn't.)

Nan sighed. "It's probably for the best, having everything out in the open. I don't have to live in fear of you finding out anymore."

"And Old Lady Griggs doesn't have to be afraid of being skinned alive."

CHAPTER 20

NAN SLAMMED around the kitchen for the rest of the morning, washing and rewashing the dishes. She pulled the fridge from the wall and scrubbed the nooks and crannies, all the while griping about Griggs. "And the pot and pan band?" She sat on her haunches and dipped the scrub brush into the floor pail.

"We had a couple practices, but she's got a tin ear."

"I should have known better. That woman's tongue is hinged in the middle, never was able to keep anything quiet for long." She went back to scrubbing the floor. "But there's no use crying over spilt milk. She's told you where you come from, and what's done is done."

Nan was angry, but she still didn't know the worst of it. She didn't know that Griggs had shown me my comic strip. By the time Nan finished, the kitchen shone, the curtains were washed and starched, and tea towels were pressed and put away. "There," she said. "That was a job that needed doing." She was just about to throw the floor water out the screen door, when Old Lady Griggs came scurrying up the walk.

"Molly," she waved. "I thought we might have a talk."

Nan pushed open the door and let loose the water, narrowly missing Griggs. "Why would you want to do that, Dorigen? Hasn't there been enough talk?"

Griggs gaze fell to me. "Who's been doing the talking?"

"Oh, I don't know," Nan said. "Why don't you tell me?"

Griggs didn't say anything, she just stood there blinking her patchy eyelashes. I wanted to tell her that kind of thing only worked on Mr. Griggs, but thought it best to keep my thoughts to myself. Besides, I figured she was planning on waiting Nan out, but Nan was having none of it. She tipped her pail so it dripped on Griggs' shoe. With a sniff, Nan shut the screen door and went back into the kitchen. I curtsied and followed her. Griggs must have believed the minister when he said confession was good for the soul, because the door had hardly banged shut when Griggs pushed her face up against the screen. She pushed so hard that I thought she might rip the newly-mended hole. That would be bad. Nan had been cross when she came home from work and saw the rent. She took out her needle and thread, her lips getting tighter with every stitch she made. "And how did this happen, Celia Canterberry?"

The toe of my shoe dug into the linoleum. "Billy Billboson said at his church people get born again and I was wondering what that felt like. So I baby-body pushed myself through a little hole in the screen."

"Figures," she said.

Now that Griggs was pushing on the mesh those fine stitches might tear free and, well, the baby-body excuse wasn't going to work twice.

"Molly," Griggs said, "is that anyway to treat a neighbour?"

Nan didn't say anything, she pulled open the tea-towel drawer, pulled out a stack and started to re-iron them.

"Are you going to invite me in? I don't know if you're aware, but leaving someone standing on your doorstep is considered rude."

"Go stand somewhere else then," Nan called over her shoulder.

Griggs' face pushed harder into the screen, forming the mesh around her sharp features. "I wore my honeymoon hat."

"Must be a special occasion."

I looked back towards the screen door. "It's on backwards."

"Makes no difference," Nan said with a snicker.

Griggs screeched, "I brought my infamous frozen casserole."

Nan didn't say a word. I know she was contemplating that casserole. No other dish in the history of mankind had been frozen and thawed as much as the one Griggs held in her hands. She had offered it at every funeral and fundraiser, had even brought it to Abraham Leibowitz's bar mitzvah. In the past ten years no one had taken her up on the offer, so back in the freezer it went. Nan put down the iron, and high-stepped it to the door. "Thank you for your thoughtfulness," she said as she swung open the door and grabbed at the dish.

Griggs tightened her grip. "Are you sure you like shepherd's pie?"

"My favourite." Nan licked her tight lips and yanked.

"It's been so long since I've made it, might have lost the recipe." Griggs yanked back.

"A blessing to us all." Nan pulled.

"I made it before Mr. Griggs was stuffed and fluffed." Griggs pulled back.

"Aged like a good wine."

Griggs grimaced and let go of the casserole, causing Nan to stumble backwards. "Is that all you wanted?" Nan asked, holding the pie at arm's length.

"Now that you've asked," Griggs said, a little pitchy. "It wasn't my fault, I swear. Ask my husband. He's beside himself."

Nan huffed, and Griggs opened the screen door and followed her into the kitchen, plopping down on Nan's best chrome chair, the one I hadn't cut the vinyl on, to free the lovely cotton fluff to make dust bunny beds. "These are difficult times Molly, as you know."

"Get to the point."

"There are so many points. Which one would you like me to get to first?"

"The one that would get you skinned alive."

"Oh, that one." Griggs cleared her throat and examined her nails. "In my defence," she said after a time, "I did it for free."

"For free!" Nan's temper boiled over. She picked up her iron and waved it through the air as if she would brain Griggs at any moment. I plopped down on the chair next to Griggs. If I watched real close I might see Griggs' eyes right themselves. Tommy Harken said that sometimes happens with a really good head injury. "And you think that makes it right?" Nan continued, the iron getting menacingly close.

"Excuse me, Miss High-and-Mighty! Who else would mind her out of the goodness of their heart?" She paused, leaving time for Nan to reply, but Nan said nothing. "I thought not. And then you attack me for it."

Nan set the iron down and took a breath.

"As I was saying." Griggs fixed one eye on me, the other on Nan. "If I'd known they were here, rummaging through your things, I would have never sent her home. It's just that she was asking questions about that *man*."

"Is that the only question she's asked?"

"What are you implying?"

"I'm not implying anything, Dorigen Griggs, and you know it!"

"I don't know anything, Molly Canterberry, and I'm feeling rather hurt that you'd insist I do."

Nan rolled her eyes as she turned the range as high as it would go, picked up the casserole and slipped it inside the oven.

"You're going to heat that up now?" Griggs' face grew blotchy, as if it wasn't sure if it should get all hot and feverish or go pale and pass out. "No one heats it up."

"What else am I going to feed you?"

Griggs shrunk, and her voice came out in a whisper. "I'm not hungry."

"You damn well better be," I said for Nan, because at this point I could almost read her thoughts. "Or she'll pry your lips open herself. Won't you, Nan?"

Nan grunted but didn't disagree. Even better, she didn't yell at me for swearing. That very fact alone opened up a world of possibilities. I thought I might use *hell* next, work my way up to *son-of-a-bitch*. Those were the words Nan used when she was at the end of her rope. She never used *snot* or *fart*, she said they weren't real words and not worth the breath they took up.

I watched the back and forth between Griggs and Nan but never found an opportune time to slip in my unused vocabulary. The two were talking around what really bothered them, skipping from Griggs' inability to keep secrets to herself, to Nan's unreasonable expectations, but not once did the subject of the black scrapbook Griggs kept under the plastic-covered chesterfield come up. It wasn't until Mr. Sneaky Walker Douglas knocked on the screen door that I got my chance. I shot from my spot at the kitchen table before Nan had a chance to stop me. "Son-of -a-bitch," I said, opening the screen door, a large measure of cheer in my voice. "What the hell are you doing here?"

Nan's hard shoe steps sounded behind me and she clipped me so hard on the back of the head I almost lost my balance. "That's enough from you, Celia Canterberry," she said. Her tone sent a shiver down my spine. "I'll deal with you later." She turned to Mr. Douglas. "Won't you come in?"

He nodded and stepped through the open door. The aroma of Griggs' casserole was starting to fill the room and it was hard not to gag. I knew it must be killing Nan that such a stench was permeating her kitchen, but she stood there in the middle of her black and white checked floor acting like nothing was out of the ordinary.

"What's that gawd awful smell?" Griggs asked. "It's making my eyes burn."

"That would be your shepherd's pie," Nan said through gritted teeth.

Griggs guffawed. "Never smelt like that until you got a hold of it."

I thought Nan was going to lose her mind, but she kept her thoughts to herself. Instead, she leaned over and kissed Cobweb Sneaky Walker Walter Douglas square on the cheek. Both Griggs and I gasped. Cobweb Sneaky Walker just stood there and took it.

"Walter," Nan said, running her hand down his cheek, where the kiss had been, "I don't think I can thank you enough."

Walter didn't seem to know how she could thank him either. He just stood there nodding at Nan and then at me, just like he'd done the day my should-have-beens rifled through the house. He didn't nod at Griggs though; it was like she wasn't even there. After he made his nodding rounds, he turned and left.

"That's the most emotion I've seen from Walter in a long time." Griggs tapped her chin with her forefinger. "It's kind of nice to see that man's not made of stone. I bet he'll sic his mangy cat on those no-accounts if they dare show up here again."

"I hope so," Nan said, watching out the kitchen window as Sneaky Walker ambled back to his side of the hedge.

"Are you going to phone the R.C.M.P.?" Griggs asked.

"I suppose I should," Nan said, her eye on the hedge Sneaky Walker had disappeared behind. "But I don't think they'll take Walter seriously, let alone the word of a little girl."

"I already phoned them," I explained. "And Sneak— Mr. Douglas wouldn't speak to them. He was scared of their guns. He was shaking. And when I told them about the earthworms they rolled their eyes and left."

Nan had barely acknowledged them when Mayor Forde slipped in with The Ladies of the Perpetual Indigence Society. They didn't even knock or wipe their feet on the mat. "We're here," Mayor Forde announced as if we'd been waiting our whole lives for him to make an appearance.

"So you are," Nan crossed her arms and tapped her foot. "I don't remember extending an open invitation."

Mayor Forde didn't seem to notice her hostility. "You didn't, but that's what happens when you live in a supportive community." He smiled and bowed slightly at the waist. The Ladies of the Perpetual Indigence Society did the same.

"Remind me to move," Nan said in a voice so soft I was pretty sure I was the only one who heard.

The visitors began making their way around the room, hands neatly folded behind their backs. They opened cupboards, ran fingers along windowsills, even opened the refrigerator and smelled the milk. Nan protested each intrusion, but there were too many of them. As she slammed one cupboard shut, another was opened, like a clown car at the circus. If Nan hadn't been so upset, I might have opened a few doors myself.

Mayor Forde scratched his belly. "Everything in good order, ladies?"

The PIS ladies grunted in unison.

"Just as I told you, Miss Canterberry wouldn't let us down. Would you, Molly?" He undid the only button on his black and yellow striped bumblebee suit jacket that hadn't popped off, letting his belly expand naturally. His lilac-coloured flowered shirt was doing its level best to hold back what his lazy skin had long ago given up on. I went to the pot and pan cupboard and picked out the biggest lid I could find. If one of those rascally buttons broke free, the force alone could cause permanent damage, and I wanted to be prepared. On the bright side, if a button did fly, Mr. Griggs would have his third eye, making him the only mystic in Happy Valley.

The more I tried, the more I couldn't keep my eyes off those buttons and the bloops of skin exposed between each one, like petals of a flower. Then I spotted it: the cavernous hole of a belly-button. It occurred to me that a small rodent could take refuge there, make a nest of the belly button lint. Mayor Forde wouldn't even notice. Nan said he was oblivious to most things, and could hardly remember he was on his fifth wife. Lucky for him they all had the same first name: Woman.

As for The Ladies of the Perpetual Indigence Society, they were huddled together like a choir ready to sing an out-of-season Christmas carol. With hankies pressed tight against their up-turned noses, they tried to escape the stench of Griggs' heating casserole. Mrs. Whitford lowered her hanky and spoke for the group. "The mayor asked us to attend. He said it was our civic duty."

"Mmm hmm," Nan said, her jaw set tight.

"With Mayor Forde's new revitalization package," Mrs. Whitford continued, "the one he proposed at the last town council meeting, that little girl of yours is going to bring more than her fair share of financial benefits to our little community, and for that we wanted to express our thanks. And make sure her living conditions are adequate, of course."

Nan got a funny look in her eye. She walked over to the stove, popped it open and began pumping the door, making sure no one missed the unpalatable stench. The PIS Ladies gasped and didn't even try to hide their gags. "What proposal?" Nan asked.

"Nothing to worry your pretty little head about," Mayor Forde said, coughing.

I don't think anyone in Nan's whole life had told her not to worry her pretty little head. Mayor Forde was the first, and by the look on Nan's face, I was pretty sure he'd be the last.

"Molly," one of the PIS ladies interjected. "I look forward to what that granddaughter of yours will do next. It's the only reason I buy the paper anymore."

Nan banged melamine plates and cutlery on the table, like she was awash in them and didn't care a lick if any ended up cracked or broke. "Is that so? It's the only reason I don't."

The ladies either didn't notice or didn't care that they were making Nan uncomfortable in her own home. Mrs. Whitford, the centre of their tight knot, cleared her throat.

Griggs tapped me on the shoulder as her lazy eye wobbled with excitement. "She's going to make an articulation. I hope your Nan clobbers her."

Mrs. Whitford cleared her throat again and addressed the PIS ladies instead of Nan. "Miss Canterberry works for me you know. And although I find her work just shy of adequate," she wrinkled her nose, "my husband says we can't do without her."

Griggs and I looked slumped shoulders at each other. "That wasn't worth clearing her throat for," I said.

Griggs nodded in agreement.

"I think she's still upset about the permanent Jiffy marker. Nan said she hasn't stopped going on about it. Hears about it every time she enters the building."

"You're preaching to the choir," Griggs said. "She'd best put up her dukes, cause the fur is going to fly." The two of us hunkered down and waited for the carnage.

Nan pulled the casserole from the oven and placed it on a hotpad on the centre of the table. With her biggest serving spoon, she scooped out a large portion, plopped it on a plate and thrust the plate towards Mrs. Whitford.

"I'm not hungry," Mrs. Whitford said, slipping back in the PIS pack.

"In my kitchen everyone eats," Nan insisted.

"You first."

"That would be rude."

They were at an impasse. Mrs. Whitford wasn't going to partake, and Nan wasn't going to relent. Griggs and I sat on the sidelines, forgotten. It was delightful. "I'll get a fork," I said. "And some milk to wash it down."

"It will take a lot more than milk to wash that down," Nan said. For every step she took forward, Mrs. Whitford and her gaggling feather heads took a step back. It wasn't long until Nan had herded the group out the door and off the step.

CHAPTER 21

WHILE NAN WAS busy dealing with The Ladies of the Perpetual Indigence Society on the front step, Mayor Forde spread the Happy Valley Journal on her clean kitchen floor. "We have to hurry, before your Nan returns." He reached for Griggs' casserole dish and helped himself to a large spoonful. After a pause, a look of concern crossed his face. "Did Molly make this?" he said, speaking around the slop.

Griggs shook her head, and with a self-satisfied smile pointed a thumb towards herself.

"Thought as much," Mayor Forde said, opening his mouth and returning the offending gob back into the dish. "Fit for neither man nor beast."

Griggs huffed. "Well if you were a man I might think you had a point."

Mayor Forde dismissed Griggs with a wave of his hand. "I didn't come by tonight to discuss your casserole. I came by to congratulate Miss Celia here. The future of Happy Valley is looking up because of her. It's going to be the best year ever, businesses are going to boom." His eyebrows waggled. "Since my plan has been announced, folks from miles around are lining up to get their pictures taken on our sidewalk stars. Came by just to make sure you were on board."

"Those stars have been around for forever and a day," Griggs said. "Why would anyone take notice of them now?"

"Haven't you been paying attention? Mr. Whitford has sent away for a map to identify how each star corresponds to a comic strip episode. Going to sell them at the drugstore. That's what we've been missing. The stars meant nothing without a map to identify them." Mayor Forde waved his hands in the air like a mime. "'Come stand where she stood. Pose and snap a picture just like the comic strip foundling.'" The man beamed. "And Frank Murray is going to do his part as well, set aside a corner of his haberdashery for costume rentals. 'Dress like the waif.'"

Griggs looked a little horrified. "No one told me, and I know no one has talked about it with Molly, she'd have mentioned it."

"Town council had a meeting and decided it was easier to ask forgiveness than permission."

"She wouldn't grant either."

"That's why we're not going to ask her." He looked back towards the screen door nervously. "Can you imagine our streets filled with all your comic strip readers re-enacting the best parts of your life?"

"No," I said.

"Just try."

I could tell by the look on Griggs' face she didn't approve. Probably because she'd not thought of it. Mayor Forde pulled a mocked up map from his jacket pocket. "Here," he said, pointing to a star in front of the post office. "This is where Celia stripped down to her altogether, when Molly was inside buying stamps. And here," he pointed to a different star, "is where Celia claimed she heard Mrs. Jasmin's long dead husband." He looked down at me. "Do you remember that Celia?"

I shook my head.

He leaned back and licked his thick lips. "It's quite a story. Mrs. Jasmin's bakery sign was outdated. *Grab My Buns Bakery* doesn't draw the patrons when the baker is in her seventies. Hence the change to *Saggy Buns Bakery*."

I didn't remember the old sign, but ever since the new one had been hammered up Mrs. Jasmin greeted each customer, familiar or not, with the same quip: "Don't even ask. It happens with age." Some days we just went in to make her say it, so Nan could have a good chuckle.

"Why are you telling us things we already know?" Griggs' voice was sharp, so I knew she was frustrated. She wanted to talk about Oswald Elliot and his ineptitude, not Mrs. Jasmine and her migrating buttocks.

Mayor Forde's weeping eyes turned on Griggs. They looked her up and down with such disregard I thought she'd throttle him with her honeymoon hat. "It's all part of the dance I call 'Self-promotion.'"

Griggs rolled her eyes, one at a time.

"As I was saying," Mayor Forde continued, "Celia, no bigger than a minute, pointed up at the bakery's new sign and proclaimed, *He doesn't like it, he doesn't like it at all*." Mayor Forde stepped out of his memory and addressed me. "It was your first public declaration and so, as you can imagine, it carried a fair amount of water. Most didn't know you could speak, let alone string half a dozen words together. It was like you were possessed."

I wasn't sure what to think; Griggs hadn't showed me any of the comic strips he was talking about. Made me a little disappointed in her, leaving me unprepared like this. The only thing I could think to do was let out a deep sigh and scrunch my shoulders. The gelatinous mayor could interpret it any way he liked.

Mayor Forde licked his lips again, and pulled a wad of

newspaper clippings from his inside jacket pocket. He rummaged through the bundle. "Here it is," he said, straightening it on the kitchen table. He set the cream and sugar set on opposite corners to hold the crinkled mess down. *"Miss Canterberry stops short. She's out for a Sunday stroll, not to cause a scene or draw any unwanted attention, but her underling has other intentions. The young thing drools, dragging one ape-like arm. When coming abreast of the bakery the foundling raises her abnormal appendage and grunts, 'Mr. Jasmin doesn't like it, he doesn't like it at all.'"*

Griggs flushed. "Mr. Jasmin is no longer with us, and I don't think it's decent to speak of him in such a way."

"Need I remind you, Dorigen, being dead didn't stop his corpse from whispering into the foundling's ear." Mayor Forde scoffed and continued reading. *"The crowd turns as if their heads are on swivels. 'She doesn't know what she's saying,' Miss Canterberry stammers, trying to grab hold of her offspring's offspring and slip back into the crowd, but it is too late, the bell has been rung. Mrs. Jasmin, who has been holding weekly séances since her husband's demise, turns on the youngest Canterberry. 'Why doesn't he like it?' she cries desperately.*

The little demon shakes her head and totters off into the crowd, her grandmother in close pursuit."

Mayor Forde looked up from the scrap of paper. "It was your first premonition. No more than a week after the sign was hung it came toppling down, almost decapitating Agnes Obermeyer."

"She wasn't nearly decapitated," Griggs scoffed.

"She would have been," Mayor Forde protested, "if she'd come downtown an hour earlier and was on the bakery side of the street."

Griggs was probably vibrating inside. It took so little for

some to find their way into my cartoon strip, while others like herself hardly got a mention.

"Folks didn't go back to the bakery for at least a week," Mayor Forde went on. "Not until the front window's glass was replaced, thus freeing Mr. Jasmin's spirit that was trapped within."

"It was Doc Marley's idea to change the glass," Griggs chimed in. "He said in the old country that kind of thing happened all the time. And it was much easier changing a pane than burning the witch that had cursed it."

"Doc Marley never said that." Mayor Forde seemed to be growing weary of Griggs' interruptions.

"He didn't have to, it was implied."

"Implied when?"

"When he said the whole thing gave him the heebie-jeebies."

"God, some days I swear..." Mayor Forde reddened. "The only reason the sign fell was because your shiftless brother-in-law hung it." She pursed her lips. "That and the window glass. You can never be too careful about those things."

"As I was saying," Mayor Forde went on, ignoring Griggs' comment, "a map is being made, with stars indicating all of Celia's strange interactions. Gonna sell it along with the road maps."

"That's reprehensible," Griggs said, probably realizing her one and only chance of getting a star had gone out the window when she had sent me home for asking about Nan's honeymoon hat.

"Can't argue with you about that. But do you know how popular that cartoon has become? Compared to all of the other burgeoning businesses in Happy Valley, that's the scheme that shows the most promise."

I was starting to agree with Griggs. That map wasn't a very

good idea. If strangers were going to come to town and act out comic strip scenarios, there would be a whole slew of arrests.

Mayor Forde seemed to sense our lack of enthusiasm, so he quickly changed the subject. "But my primary reason for coming by was to go over this latest strip with you, Celia." He leaned over and jabbed a thick finger at the first frame. "Is this the way you told it to Oswald Elliot?"

I looked from Mayor Forde to Griggs. Her arms were crossed and she was chewing the inside of her cheek. All the spit and vinegar seemed to have evaporated from her, yet she still seemed as eager as I was to examine the comic strip that Mayor Forde had spread on the kitchen floor.

I sat crossed legged on the cool black and white tiles, with Griggs hovering over my shoulder. It wasn't the same as when we sat on the plastic-covered chesterfield, all clandestine in Griggs' living room, like we were sharing government secrets and could get shot at any minute. Without that and Griggs' pencil crayon flourishes, I deflated; the whole thing seemed rather dull to me. "Rather banal, isn't it?"

"What she means," Griggs said, laying a comforting hand on my shoulder. "Is when you are so used to living your life as performance art, as Celia does, it's hard to see it bastardized."

I nodded.

Mayor Forde sucked his teeth.

Griggs and I had gone too far, and let the cat out of the bag. Now the whole town would know me and Griggs were cavorting over scrapbook pages. As Agnes Obermeyer would say, tell the mayor, tell the world. The hours Griggs and I had spent talking about my comic strip adventures, thinking no harm would come of it, were long gone.

A slow understanding crossed Mayor Forde's face. "I thought Celia only recently became aware of the strip. Apparently I was wrong." He turned to Griggs. "What have you and

Celia been up to? And more importantly, does Molly know about it?"

Griggs looked at me and raised her eyebrows. I raised my eyebrows back. It was all we needed to do, we had an understanding. She was D'Artangnan and I Porthos, we knew each other to the core. When she zigged I'd be ready to zag. My only concern was that Athos might step back into the room any minute, and she was already a little cranky for being left in the dark. She'd think the whole thing a dirty business.

As the mayor puzzled things out, there was a long, ticking-clock silence, and I could feel the hairs on the back of my neck get weary from standing at attention. I knew without even looking that Griggs' lazy eye was probably spinning around like a magic eight ball, looking for something clever to say, something that would make Mayor Forde forget why he was questioning us.

Old Lady Griggs' lazy eyed stilled, and when she finally spoke I almost held my breath. "See here," she said, skipping over Mayor Forde's inquiry and focusing on the strip that lay on the floor. Her hands were on her knees and her lip was twitching. "It's a shame he doesn't have more imagination." She pointed to the first square in the virgin strip. "Case in point, there's no ghoulie shadows or infestation of snakes. There should always be at least one of the Old Testament plagues. Things that are commonly associated with evil." Griggs flicked the paper with a jagged fingernail. "And look at the sky, not a cloud. The man can't even set a mood."

Mayor Forde's brow furrowed. "You might have a point." His black and yellow striped suit was so lively it almost moved without him. "I'll have a word with him."

"Good luck. I've been pointing out his deficiencies for years and it's gotten me nowhere."

"Well you're not the God-appointed mayor." Mayor Forde

straightened his collar. "Now let's get back to why I'm here." He looked at me. "Before your Nan gets back, I need you to tell me what really happened. Then I'll get out of your hair, but you'd better hurry. The Ladies of the Perpetual Indigence Society can only keep her occupied for so long."

I looked to Griggs who nodded; apparently she was as curious as the mayor. "Well," I said, bending a little closer to the paper strewn on the floor, "that's me on my tiptoes trying to peak through the window."

"But she wasn't wearing that dress," Griggs chimed in. "I've never seen her in such a ridiculous thing. All fancy hair and frilly socks. Only a PIS lady would dress a child like that."

Mayor Forde ignored Old Lady Griggs. "And what about here?" He pointed to another box.

"That's me holding my dust bunny. He used to guard my treasure."

Mayor Forde looked unimpressed, and I told him dust bunnies were very reliable. "They're not at all like hairballs. Hairballs have their own best interests at heart, never trust a hairball. Whereas dust bunnies are practically fearless," I said. "Dark corners, no problem, tiny spaces, works for them, and best of all, they're never tempted to pocket anything for themselves."

"Get on with it. I didn't come here to talk about your dust bunny and spiderweb circus." Mayor Forde pointed to an earlier square. "What's this?"

"Well, that's me sneaking in the squeaky screen door. I could only spit on the bottom hinge, to take the squeak out. Couldn't reach the top. So I had to tear a whole in the screen." The next box was a bit of a puzzle. It took me a minute to figure it out. The way Oswald had drawn it, I was all loopy curls and frilly dress, a damsel in distress, the kind that mustache-twirling villains tie to railroad tracks. The kind of girl, if we got a chance, me and Archibald would beat up at recess. I could stomach the pumpkin head, and the draggy arm, but a namby-pamby fainting girl? That made me throw up a bit in my mouth.

The caption read, *Out of her element, Celia Canterberry's eyelashes flutter.* "Oh my, oh my," she says, in a frozen state of petrification. "What to do, what to do?" Thoughts of her idol, Oswald Elliot, bring her to her senses. "I can do this," Celia says. "As God is my witness, I can do this, for Oswald's sake."

"I'm not like Nurse Timmer," I said. "I never fainted, and I didn't fan myself or get the vapours."

Mayor Forde flinched. "And what's wrong with Nurse Timmer? She's a fine example of a woman who knows her place. You could take a page from her book."

I felt like spitting. Griggs put her hands on my shoulders to hold me back.

"And?" Mayor Forde encouraged.

As best as I could remember, I jumped from square to square, adding the details Oswald had missed. "I told Oswald Elliot that my should-have-beens had sifted through Nan's things carefully, like they'd done it before and didn't want to get caught. But the way he'd drawn it, they'd almost ripped the paper from the walls."

"I suppose that was a bit much," Mayor Forde agreed. "But you have to admit it's more dramatic that way. And there is no better newspaperman in the county, taking on what others hardly dare to think about. He's a hero. He's the little Dutch boy, with a finger in the dam, holding back all the malcontents vying for a place in his comic strip." Mayor Forde looked directly at Griggs. "Can't imagine the pressure."

Griggs reddened. "He's been talking about me?"

"Who hasn't? Why only this week Oswald told me three other towns tried to steal him away. He's one of a kind; writing and sketching the cold hard facts."

"What towns?" Griggs asked.

"How in the hell am I supposed to know?"

"Figures."

"I don't like your tone, Mrs. Griggs. You're envious of Oswald's artistic ability, but that doesn't mean you can tarnish his reputation."

"Didn't know the man had a reputation to tarnish. He hasn't even won the Pulitzer Surprise." Griggs picked up her half-empty casserole bowl and headed for the door. As she went out, Nan came in. "You'll have to excuse me, Molly," Griggs said as she passed. "I don't like the company you keep." She looked back towards the mayor and narrowed her eyes. "Besides, I have to transfer my casserole to a smaller dish and refreeze it. Don't want anyone to think they've seen the last of it."

Nan stepped aside and was, as the rest of us, a little relieved to see the backside of that dish.

Mayor Forde almost fell off his chair as he bent down to pick up the papers he'd strewn on the floor. When he had stuffed them in his inside jacket pocket, he casually rubbed his chin and addressed me. "Celia, I want to let you know the town council is thinking of awarding you the medal of bravery." He put up his hand before Nan could protest. "I know, Molly, it's not like she ate Griggs' ungodly concoction. Eating that slop is worse than the food we serve at the Happy Valley Penitentiary. They use all my mother's old recipes, and she was a horrendous cook. It's part of our two-tier rehabilitation policy. First tier — nutrition as a punishment. Second tier — head lice make the best bedfellows." Mayor Forde leaned back in Nan's best chrome chair, as if waiting to be congratulated. No one stepped forward. I was sure one of those shiny chair legs would buckle under the strain.

Mayor Forde cleared his throat and refocused. "I just want to make sure of the facts. You knew they were here, in this house, and you still went in?"

"Yes, sir."

"Alone?"

"Yes, sir."

"And you let them take all your birthday money?"

"Yes, sir."

"You are something else, child." His sweaty hand ruffled my hair. Mayor Forde reached into his pocket and retrieved a pile of loose change. "Because of your brave sacrifice, Celia Canterberry, City Hall passed the hat, and after taking off my ten percent commission and gas money," he dumped a pile of coins on the table, "I'm proud to present you with what little remains."

That night in bed I counted my replacement birthday money. A smile slipped onto my lips. The should-have-beens may have robbed me, but I was the one who'd made the profit. Archibald had nothing on that.

CHAPTER 22

"YOO-HOO!" Old Lady Griggs announced herself at the screen door. When there was no response, she bound through the door and into the kitchen. Nan, still in her curlers and housecoat, poured them both a cup of coffee. Mid-pour she paused and looked down at the path of dried mud left in Griggs' wake. "Did you wipe your feet?"

"Of course, I did," Griggs snapped. "Do you think I was raised in a barn?"

"I hold these truths to be self-evident," Nan said, as she got up from the table and grabbed the mop to wipe up the self-evidence. "What brings you by so early?"

"Look," Griggs said, smiling as sweetly as she could. "My casserole, even though he spit the better part out, gave that man the runs for nearly a week."

Nan stopped mid-mop and I knew she was pleased. We both knew who that man was without saying; he'd sat in Nan's best chrome chair in his black and yellow bumblebee suit. "How would you know that?"

"Agnes, his personal secretary. That woman is privy to a world of oddities, and keeping track of Mayor Forde is the chief source. Even Oswald Elliot took notice." Griggs laid the latest edition of the Happy Valley Journal on Nan's chrome table.

It was the second time in a week that Nan had allowed that rag in her kitchen. She leaned onto the table and examined the strip. I took a gander with unrestrained joy. Unlike Nan, I wasn't known for my judgement.

"*The God-appointed mayor,*" Griggs read, using some of her best theatrics, "*humbled by his giving nature, regrets taking a particular interest in a certain robbery. 'I was there to comfort,' Mayor Forde says on one of his many jogs to use City Hall's luxurious facilities.*

'Comfort and advise, just like I always do. But then when I was least expecting it I was offered a piece of shepherd's pie.' Mayor Forde gags at the memory. *'And not to be rude, as some ungodly-appointed mayor would do, I partook. Only later did I discover that the unnamed creator of that atrocity had been freezing and unfreezing the same concoction since before Cain killed Abel. It was a perpetual housewarming present, church potluck staple, and bereavement offering. Sadly, I was the first one to take her up on the offer and have almost met my end as a result.'*"

"That's my shepherd's pie," Griggs gasped. "And there's me!"

Me and Nan squinted our eyes, and sure as shooting, there was Griggs. Oswald Elliot had drawn her as a black widow spider, holding a rotting corpse-casserole in one leg, as she wrapped Mr. Griggs in her cocoon web with another.

"It's not very flattering, I know," said Griggs. "But there I am, with my honeymoon hat to boot. That was the dead giveaway."

"Not very many spiders wear hats," I said.

Griggs nodded. "I've never been called an *unnamed creator* before, it's so terribly exciting. Just like Mata Hari. My hair all slick under my honeymoon hat. Slipping in and out of scandals, and leaving a trail of broken hearts." Griggs sighed, both her eyes all dreamy. "All I need is a pair of fishnet stockings."

Nan looked up from the comic strip. "Four pair, you mean. One for each of your spider legs."

"I don't think Mr. Griggs will mind the expense." Griggs fanned herself with the back of her hand. "And all this time I thought I was too much of a woman for Oswald Elliot. That he could hardly bring himself to say my name, let alone draw my visage. And now there I am, for all the world to see, because of my delightful shepherd's pie."

"No one has ever called that dish a delight."

"Delight is an understatement," Griggs agreed. "There's not a soul in Happy Valley that doesn't know about that infamous casserole. It's come to define me. And with a pair of stockings, I'd be unforgettable." Griggs was sparkling. "And believe you me, that simpering fool regrets not drawing me years ago."

Griggs patted me on the top of my head. "Sorry my dear," she said. "Upstaged by my cooking."

I wrinkled my brow and re-examined the strip. Griggs was right. I wasn't in any of the boxes. "You can fix that can't you?" I felt a bit panicky inside. What if Oswald Elliot had retired me? Traded me in for a googly-eyed woman in a honeymoon hat? Griggs didn't hear me. She was too busy basking in her own glory.

"I'd best be going," she said. "Never know who might phone or drop by. Besides, I've got to bake and age another casserole, just to be prepared."

CHAPTER 23

IT WAS by happenstance that Nan and I ran into Mrs. Willoughby and Archibald. While they were leaving the Happy Valley Druggist, their arms brimming with packages, we were collecting Nan's paycheck. Nan hadn't brought me past the druggist since the bubble gum incident, but with Griggs being too busy aging casseroles, Nan had no choice. Our cupboards were nearly bare, and Nan said she wasn't of the mind to be the Old Mother Hubbard of Happy Valley.

Mrs. Whitford must have sensed I would be tagging along and had kindly taped the paycheck to the storefront window. "That woman," Nan said, stuffing the envelope in her purse. "She can't seem to help herself, any chance to flaunt her social status."

"What social status is that?" asked Mrs. Willoughby. She rubbed her round belly, causing her flowery maternity dress to ripple.

Nan's face softened. "Fancy meeting the two of you."

"It must be our lucky day." Mrs. Willoughby ruffled my hair. "Archibald's been pestering me all week, wanting to play on your sailboat bed."

I reached over and squeezed Archibald's hand, and she squeezed my hand back. "Did you get my note?" I whispered.

She nodded. "I accept your apology."

"And?" I asked.

"And what?"

"Don't you have something to add?"

"Not really." Archibald swung my arm hard and I was tempted to pull her hair, but Nan and Mrs. Willoughby were discussing the particulars of a certain get-together that seemed a little more appealing. The thought of playing on my sailboat bed with someone besides the moody Huw thrilled me to no end. Nan looked the two of us up and down and raised an eyebrow. "Celia and Archibald could be a menacing combination. I think they had a bit of a spat the last time they got together."

"As children sometimes do," Mrs. Willoughby winked. "But I think they're over it."

After looking us over one more time, Nan agreed.

Archibald squealed and tightened her grip on my hand. It was the grip of someone who couldn't bring themselves to say 'I'm sorry.' I forgave her on the spot. "There are so many things I have to tell you," I whispered into her ear. "I'm friends with Tiberius now."

Archibald gasped louder than I'd heard her gasp before.

"We can use him in our dust bunny and spiderweb circus. Can you imagine? There's not a kid in second grade who wouldn't want to see that."

"How much can we charge?"

"Not sure. I was supposed to have my first performance at the Happy Valley Druggist but got carried away with my beauty consulting."

"I heard about that."

"Seems everybody has."

"I like my hair the way it is."

Leaning over, I touched her dusty locks. "Are you sure?" Archibald's eyes went wide and I withdrew my hand and shrugged my shoulders. "If you change your mind you know where to find me."

Nan and Mrs. Willoughby finished making the arrangements. Nan wished her luck in her upcoming delivery and Mrs. Willoughby voiced her regrets about the recent robbery. After helping to deposit the parcels in the back of the Willoughby's car, Nan turned to leave, with me and Archibald skipping merrily after her.

"All right, Captain Ahab," I said to Archibald as she climbed up on the sailboat bed beside me. "I'm Queequeg, and when Nan comes to tell us it's time for lunch, we'll pretend she's Moby Dick, and harpoon her with these willow sticks I sharpened this morning." I held out two peeled and whittled willow branches.

Archibald's jaw went slack. "She lets you do that?"

"Not on regular days, but this is a company day."

"I'd rather not," she said, refusing to take the offering. "Can we play something else?"

"Well, I could be Puck and you, Helena."

"Does Helena harpoon anyone?"

"Nope, she's not that fun, and because of it, nobody loves her. Also, she's covered with warts."

Archibald eyed the harpoon stick. "Does anyone love Captain Ahab?"

"Everyone," I said, and I answered her next question before it was even asked. "No warts."

Captain Ahab smiled as we crouched and waited for Moby Dick to ascend the stairs. The wind had let go of Pequod's sails, and the silence stilled even the bravest of hearts. Captain Ahab tightened her grip on her harpoon, and I, Queequeg, stood dutifully beside her. "It's time," said the Captain as we heard the creak of the top step.

Nan was still cross at us while we ate our macaroni and fried baloney. "It was Queequeg's idea," I said, dipping my meat into a pool of ketchup.

"It's always Queequeg's idea."

"I know, he's a nasty sort." I did a quick lick of my plate. "But what can one expect from a sailor?"

―――

It was the middle of the night when Archibald began to cry, a slow sob at first, but by the time it woke Nan it was a torrent. "What's wrong?" Nan said, sitting down on my sailboat bed and pulling Archibald into her lap. "Did Celia do something to frighten you?" Nan looked at me as if I had just slapped a baby. "Did she harpoon you too?"

Archibald shook her head.

"Then what is it?"

I poked Archibald in the ribs. Our visit had been delightful. Archibald got to throw the first spear at Moby Dick, and to hold on to the sailboat sail when a hurricane almost threw poor Queequeg overboard. What did she have to complain about?

"My mom is going to have her baby soon." Archibald's voice was as small as I've ever heard it.

Nan pulled her closer. "She'll be fine, she's done this many times."

"Five times," Archibald sniffed. "This will be her sixth."

"After five it's old hat," Nan said with a smile in her voice. "Just you wait and see."

Archibald wiped her nose on her sleeve and gulped for air. "It's not my mom I'm worried about. It's Sly Willoughby, my new father. I like him."

Nan made a deep moaning sound, and I knew she felt the

same way as Archibald. No one talked about Mrs. Willoughby's husbands when it came close to her time. If they did it would be tempting fate, calling the jaws of death to open wide and take hold of another of Archibald's fathers. The thought gave me the willies. Old Lady Griggs said only a fool would marry that woman, with the way bad luck sat in her shadow.

The three of us sat on the bed a little longer, Nan making hushing sounds and me counting the steamboats between Archibald's nose drips. After a time, in spite of Nan's hushing and rocking Archibald, the drips didn't lessen. In fact they were about half a steamboat faster.

Archibald stiffened and began to shake, but the more she shook the tighter Nan held her. If Nan's bosoms didn't suffocate her, it was only out of sheer luck. "Well, we can't telephone at this time of night, your mother has been woken up too many times by that ring, and I'm not going to be the one to cause her unnecessary worry. I'm sure we can wake one of the hired girls with a good tap on one of their bedroom windows and leave your mother to her sleep. Sound good?"

We both nodded.

"And since I don't have a car of my own, we'll have to walk." She lifted Archibald's chin with a fingertip. "Are you up for that?"

"I think so."

"Good, get your things, we'll have you home before you can say Jack Robinson." Nan looked from me to Archibald and raised her eyebrows. "It will be like Captain Ahab and Queequeg sneaking off Pequod in the middle of the night."

"During the witching hour?" I asked, the excitement growing inside me. At that moment I was kind of glad Archibald was crying. It lent more drama to our midnight adventure.

Nan rolled her eyes. "Yes, during the witching hour."

"Why are we sneaking?" I pushed Archibald off of Nan's lap and took her place.

"To get supplies before we're overtaken by pirates."

I wrinkled my nose and shook my head. "I'm not sure Captain Ahab would get his own supplies. He doesn't seem like that kind of man, being nearsighted and night blind. And as for Queequeg, he doesn't like carrying things."

"For the love of Pete, Celia, it was a suggestion, something to stir the imagination."

"It's just not very realistic, that's all."

Nan's lips tightened, and I knew she was steaming inside. As quick as I could, I pulled on Archibald's arm, and tried to hoist her back on Nan's lap, while I slid off the other side.

"How's this for realistic," Nan said, standing, nearly knocking both me and Archibald to the floor. "Oswald Elliot has been hovering around more than usual. Most likely saw us in front of the drugstore and followed us home. While you two were up here sharpening your spears, he's been crouching in the caraganas. Caught him peeking through the hallway window when I got out of the bath."

"Were you wrapped in a towel at least?"

"What kind of question is that? Of course I was."

I shrugged. "That would have made quite a strip."

"There's no talking to you," Nan said, pointing to my bedroom door. Her long index finger made a demand rather than a suggestion.

"I'm not going to Frankenstein-walk," I said, a little disappointed with her attitude. "Queequeg doesn't participate in such frivolities."

Archibald was blubbering and gulping the whole time the three of us put on our rubber boots. It didn't help that Nan refused to turn on any lights in the house. She said she didn't want to give Oswald Elliot advance notice of our intentions. We tripped and stumbled over one another trying to find our boots in the dark. By the time we were bundled up and standing on the doorstep, I'd had almost enough of our midnight adventure. The night was black as pitch, with hardly a sliver of moonlight. "Can't we use a flashlight?" I asked. "I could punch myself in the face and not even see it coming."

"No," Nan chided, ignoring half of my remark. "Draws too much attention. Besides, I've lived in Happy Valley my whole life and if I can't find my way around in the dark, I might as well be taken out and shot."

We stepped out into the night all shivery, blinking into the abyss. Nan hesitated on the step, and I knew she was rethinking our adventure. But Archibald was so determined to be with her mother, Nan didn't have a choice.

She and I trailed behind Nan, like a duo of inept ducklings; me at the rear. We slopped around in our rubber boots, each holding on to the tail of the coat ahead of us. "Archibald," I whispered. "Do you want to trade me places?"

In the dim moonlight I could barely see her shake her head. I scrunched my shoulders around my ears, to keep away any neck breathers, the ones that follow small children in the dark and use their dragon breath to cook them without them even knowing it. "It's just that Nan has a bad habit of farting when she's stressed."

Archibald tucked in closer behind Nan, as if her farting was something to look forward to. And then, out of the blue, Archibald began to sing some snivelling verse of Jesus Loves Me. The little Sunday School song was punctuated with snot bubbles, the very thing that attracted neck breathers. Their siren call.

"It smells like rain," I said, trying to distract myself.

"There's been a promise of rain all day," Nan said over Archibald's caterwauling. "It's come to nothing so far, and there is no need for us to worry about it now." She pulled at her overcoat, and looked down at us. "No time for chitchat. If we don't get a move on, Archibald is going to dehydrate."

I looked at Archibald. From what I could see in the squinty moonlight, she was getting rather limpy. "You know Archibald," I said, "with all your blubbering you're gonna look like Griggs. Doc Marley said that's exactly how she got her lazy eye."

Archibald didn't take the news well. Her blubbering turned to wailing and no matter what Nan said, she couldn't calm her. Nan finally gave up and told me to keep my mouth shut. "She's the one singing about Jesus. All I did was give a health warning."

Nan huffed. "I don't know why I ever thought you having a friend over was a good idea."

We didn't say much after that, though Archibald kept singing. She knew more verses than I cared to listen to. Nan didn't lead us down the expected places, like the sidewalks or the usual shortcuts. Nan seemed to think they were too predictable. Instead, we made a beeline through Farmer Hempel's cow pasture. Nan's house and Mrs. Willoughby's were at kitty corner ends of the thing, that is if you didn't count the three back alleys and Cobweb Sneaky Walker's side yard we had to traverse first. We were halfway through the pasture when the promise of rain became a reality, pelting us and making every blinks-eyed step more hazardous than the one before. Just about the time I was nearly soaked through, I heard it. Not very loud at first, but it was there just the same.

Archibald stopped short. "What was that?"

"Witches," I said, knowing full well it was the sound of a squeaky-wheeled bicycle. I'd spied it tucked under the edge of Nan's box hedge earlier in the day and thought nothing of it until Nan told me Oswald Elliot was using the hedge as a hideout. Oswald Elliot and his indispensable banana-seat bike. Most of the commotion didn't happen until we were on the other side of Farmer Hempel's barbed wire fence. But it was hard to tell where it was coming from. With the pounding rain and the bawling cattle, I could hardly hear Archibald's singing.

She stopped mid-verse and turned to me. "There it was again. Did you hear it?"

"Witches," I repeated, hoping I was wrong and it was just Oswald Elliott on his rickety banana-seat bike. But telling Archibald it was just Oswald might mean she'd quit singing her Jesus song, and where would that leave me at the back of the line?

"When it rains," I whispered to Archibald, "like it is now, and the moon is so scared it only shows a sliver of its face, witches ditch their brooms and pick up their bicycles."

"They do not," she said in a voice that was doing its best not to scream.

"Don't believe me, that's fine and dandy. You're not the one at the back of the line, you're safe and sound, snug behind my Nan and her farty bum. I'm the canary in the coalmine."

"What's that supposed to mean?"

"You'll see."

Archibald tucked closer to Nan. "I don't like witches."

I didn't like witches either, did I, but I didn't say anything. "Just keep singing," I said. "Witches hate singing."

Archibald took a big gulp of air and started the next verse. I looked to the dark shapes of Archibald and Nan, thinking it might be the last time I almost saw them. A lump grew in my throat. The sooner we got out of Farmer Hempel's pasture the better. That's when the lightning flashed and Archibald screamed. One of Farmer Hempel's wild roan cows lost her mind and went barrelling past, snorting with her head lowered. If Oswald Elliot's bicycle had a squeak before, it would have a twist to match it now.

CHAPTER 24

I HADN'T BEEN VISITING at the Willoughby's for a couple of husbands. Not since Archibald's fourth birthday, when I accidentally singed Sally Shepard's moustache trying to relight the birthday candles. It wasn't my fault, but the way everyone carried on it was as if I'd threatened her at gunpoint. After that Archibald only had "family" birthday parties.

It had been a relief to Nan; she said my ears were too twitchy to go to other people's houses, and the other people who lived in those houses had tongues that were too waggy. Since Griggs had shown me the scrapbook, I agreed with her.

Before we'd started out on our midnight adventure I'd guessed that Archibald's house had changed since the birthday party. Archibald said it started out small but each time one of her fathers died, her mother added a new room. The lightning flashed, and sure as shooting, Archibald was right, the house *was* bigger. It was a Frankenstein monster of a house, with added bits that didn't look like they belonged. I loved the ambience.

"All right," Nan said, looking down at Archibald. "Which is one of the hired girl's windows?"

Archibald's shaky hand pointed. The window wasn't very far from where we stood, not very high up, perfect for knocking.

Nan stepped into the muddy flowerbed and began tapping. That's when the screaming began. At first I thought it was Archibald, but she had started a whole new Jesus Loves Me verse at the top of her voice, as if she were trying to drown out the screams.

The screaming had come from *inside* the house.

Apparently, Mrs. Willoughby's hired girl didn't like her window banged on in the middle of the night during a lightning storm. Nan put her face against the window pane, making soothing sounds like she had when she'd tried to comfort Archibald on my bed. The screaming got worse, and the silly girl started throwing things. "You'll wake the dead," Nan shouted at the glass. Which, in turn, only made Archibald sing louder.

With talk of witches, dead people waking, and cows charging in the pasture, Archibald had had about as much as she could take. That's when we heard the sound of someone pumping a shotgun. Mrs. Willoughby flipped on the porch light and flung open the front door. She'd been roused by the hired girl's screams.

"Who's out there?" she yelled into the storm.

Nan stepped in front of me and Archibald. She had the same look on her face as when Captain Ahab harpooned her. "I've got your daughter."

Mrs. Willoughby leaned out the door frame. Her face was white and drawn and she didn't seem pleased to find the three of us standing there. "What the…"

When Archibald saw her mother she bolted around Nan and threw her arms around Mrs. Willoughby's waist. I was a little shocked that Mrs. Willoughby looked well rested for a soon-to-be-widow.

"Archibald!" she cried, waving us in.

As we traipsed in, Nan leaned over and warned me. "Keep it down," she said. "We've wakened one Willoughby, there is no need to wake anymore."

I wanted to remind her Archibald's little siblings weren't all Willoughbys, but she didn't look like she was in the mood for reminding.

Mrs. Willoughby leaned her shotgun against the wall before bending down to cup her daughter's cheeks. "What on earth?" It was as if they hadn't seen each other in weeks. Archibald wept out sounds that weren't even words, and when she was done, Mrs. Willoughby turned to Nan. She gave her such a look, I was surprised Nan didn't die on the spot. I'd never seen Nan shrink like that before.

"We didn't want to wake you," Nan started, with a bit of a stutter. "But Archibald insisted on coming home."

Mrs. Willoughby didn't say anything for a long time. She was too busy taking in the whole of us dripping on her porch floor. Nan wasn't looking her best, and Archibald and me were no better, her in two right footed rubber boots and me in two left footed ones. Pushing my hair out of my eyes, I curtsied and bowed my head a little. I hadn't been to the Willoughby's since that unfortunate birthday, and I wanted to make a good impression. Nan wasn't much for social graces, and left the whole thing up to me. I looked up at Mrs. Willoughby and smiled. "The only reason why we haven't been killed by witches is because of Archibald's Jesus Loves Me song. You should be very proud."

Archibald nodded.

Nan closed her eyes, and I knew she was counting to ten by the way she was taking deep breaths.

Mrs. Willoughby blinked as if she wasn't sure how to take the news. "Since I'm up, I might as well make a pot of tea. We'll get things sorted out."

"Oh, that won't be necessary," Nan said. "We should be getting back."

"Don't be ridiculous." Mrs. Willoughby shivered as she looked past us to the pelting rain. "I wouldn't send a dog out there."

Archibald had quit sniffling and was smiling from ear to ear. "A midnight tea party," she whispered, her eyes all puffy. "It's ever so exciting."

I nodded, this was almost as much fun as harpooning. We both sat down to slip off our boots, leaving puddles of rainwater on the tiled floor. I tried to wipe it up with my socks but they were already dripping wet. The puddle expanded until it covered most of the porch floor.

"Stop that," Nan said, a bit sharply. "You're making a mess."

"I'm not trying to."

I wanted to tell her that she was one to talk. Nan had never looked so unattractive in her life. It was rather embarrassing. Hair all flattened to her head, overcoat hanging lopsided as if she had peeled it off of a drunk rodeo clown who'd been trampled by a bull. Not very appropriate for an adult left in charge of two small children, and *she* had the nerve to stand there and complain about me?

Mrs. Willoughby left the room and returned with an armful of towels. She told me and Archibald to strip down to our skivvies, and she'd throw our things into the new dryer. Nan smirked. Mrs. Willoughby handed Nan her biggest towel without any instructions; apparently Nan was to fend for herself.

Wrapped in our towels, Archibald and me stepped into a kitchen with a blue and white checkered floor, perfect for hop-scotch. It was like stepping into one of the glossy-paged magazines I had seen at the Happy Valley Druggist. A matching Frigidaire refrigerator and stove, a sunburst wall clock, and a pop down toaster were just some of the amenities. I brought my hands to my throat; a pop down toaster! Nan toasted our bread on a cookie sheet in the oven, scraping off the blackened edges before buttering the thick slabs. A pop down toaster would be almost as good as store-bought bread. I wanted to clap my hands with glee but didn't think Nan would approve.

When the tea was finally served, Nan and Mrs. Willoughby hadn't said much. Their chairs scraped the floor and their teaspoons clicked against the sides of the china cups. Watching the two of them sent shivers down my spine. I jabbed Archibald in the ribs. "It's just like Wuthering Heights," I said. "Nan read me that book a while ago. She's the brooding Heathcliff and your mother is the resentful Hindley." I began swinging my legs. "You can be Catherine and I can be the maid, Nelly."

Archibald looked a bit uncomfortable. "Do I have to spear anyone?"

"No," I said. "But you have to marry someone you don't love."

Archibald frowned.

"He's rich."

"Okay."

Archibald and me sipped our tea. I called her Miss and dabbed anything that dribbled down her chin with a napkin. Archibald seemed to be dribbling on purpose. "You're going to make me rub your chin raw," I said.

"Nelly." Archibald raised an eyebrow. "Do you want to keep your job?"

How was I supposed to answer that? Nelly would never talk back to Catherine Earnshaw. I swung my legs harder and looked from Heathcliff to Hindley. I didn't like Miss Catherine Earnshaw at the moment. "Where's Mr. Willoughby?" I asked.

Mrs. Willoughby looked down at her teacup. "He'll be

home in the morning. He promised he'd pull over if the weather took a turn."

"And I'm sure he did." Nan patted the back of her hand.

The smile that crossed Mrs. Willoughby's face wasn't much of a smile at all. And I knew she must be as worried as Archibald was, sobbing into a pillow and singing Jesus Loves Me until all the words were just a jumble of noise. I didn't blame her, all those husbands dying with neither rhyme nor reason.

Nan gave Mrs. Willoughby an apologetic smile. "I'm so sorry," she said.

"So am I." Mrs. Willoughby looked at her hands and changed the subject. "What happened to the three of you?"

"Oh, I think Archibald was missing you." Nan's eyes were gentle. "She couldn't sleep and wanted to come home."

I rolled my eyes. Nan was leaving out all the best parts. "Excuse me, that's not how I remember it." I tapped the table with a fingertip. "You came into my bedroom, got us out of bed, and said we were going on a midnight run. Said we were going to get supplies before some wayward pirates could skin us alive." I paused. "And we were being chased by witches."

Archibald nodded profusely, the fear of everything that had happened coming back into her eyes. Her pale skin turned even more pale, and she threw up.

Leaning over, I rubbed her back; a maid's work was never done. "Catherine Earnshaw doesn't have a very strong stomach, has always been a bit of a bleeder." I kissed her on the forehead. Catherine was lucky to have a maid as loyal as Nelly.

It was Nan who cleaned up Archibald's sick. And when her mouth was close to my ear she whispered, "I knew the two of you were an unlucky combination."

I kept rubbing Catherine's back, ignoring Heathcliff. What else could I do? I didn't have the means to escape his treachery.

"I think it's time to turn in. Everyone has had enough excitement for one night," Mrs. Willoughby said, stifling a yawn.

Nan nodded and motioned for me to follow her, and we started for the front door. My heart sank, for the rain had picked up and was coming down so heavy it was drowning everything in sight. If there hadn't been witches before, I was sure there were witches now. They were probably pounding on the windows to get in.

"Where do you think you're going? You'll have to bunk here," Mrs. Willoughby said as we reached for our boots. "Celia, you crawl into bed with Archibald, and Molly, I'll make up the davenport for you."

"We don't want to put you out," Nan said.

"You're not, not on a night like this." Mrs. Willoughby almost sounded relieved. "It'll be good to know the house is full."

The hired girl, who looked a lot like Isabella Linton, came out of her back bedroom. It took a little of my breath away. She made the sign of the cross when she looked at Nan, narrowing her eyes. Mrs. Willoughby sent her to fetch sheets and blankets. It was hard not to gasp, someone so high and mighty in such a lowly position. I wanted to reach out and touch her. She looked a bit resentful, likely from being scared to death from Nan yelling and pounding on her bedroom window in a lightning storm, and then having to mop up after us.

"We'll wait out the storm together," Mrs. Willoughby said, interrupting my musings.

Lightning cracked and the whole outside lit up through the porch door window. Through squinted eyes I swear Oswald Elliot was lugging his mangled bicycle up Mrs. Willoughby's driveway. A plaid and argyle mess if ever there was one. The lightning cracked again, and he was gone. It made my heart jump a bit.

Mrs. Willoughby rubbed the small of her back and looked towards the black window. "Anyone out there now will catch their death of cold."

I was pretty sure if Nan knew Oswald Elliot was the one catching his death she'd bolt all the doors and sleep well in spite of it. I followed Isabella up to Archibald's bedroom. "How the mighty have fallen," I whispered in her ear as she added more blankets to the bed. She looked down at me as if I were out of my mind, but I knew it was a ruse. "My heart hurts for you."

Isabella didn't say anything, and I knew we had an understanding. I'd pass her a note at breakfast.

CHAPTER 25

ARCHIBALD SHARED A ROOM. "You sleep in the middle," she said, drawing back the top sheet.

I looked from her to the sleeping lump. "Why?" I asked, a little suspicious.

"Witches," Archibald said. "If they come through the door they'll get me first, the window, they'll get Buttons."

Buttons wasn't the Willoughby's cat. He was Archibald's younger brother. Buttons Malloy was named after his father just like Archibald was named after hers. Archibald Quigley. I crawled onto the squeaky bed, not sure how I felt about sleeping between two people.

"When you and your Nan walked me home," Archibald turned off the light and slipped onto the bed after me, "you let me be in the middle, now I'm doing you the same favour."

"That was nice of me wasn't it?" I said into the dark.

"It was. And this is nice of me too, isn't it?"

"Yes it is."

"Except," Archibald said with a yawn, "Nan's bum only farts, Buttons pees."

For most of the night I tried to stay away from Buttons and

his oozing bottom, but the little scamp kept rolling into me. It was exhausting. I laid there wondering if I was hot and sweaty from being sandwiched between two heaters, or pee soak. When I heard the pounding it was almost a relief. "They're here," I said, shaking Archibald awake.

She rubbed her eyes and whimpered. "Who's here?"

"Not sure, could be witches, who's to say?"

I could feel Archibald stiffen beside me.

"It's going to be all right," I said. "We'll check it out together." After a bit of tugging, I got Archibald out of bed and the two of us slipped down the stairs hand in hand, shivering as we went. It seemed to take forever; Archibald balked on each step. "Honestly, sometimes you make the worst Captain Ahab."

"I thought I was Catherine Earnshaw?"

"Catherine wouldn't sneak out of bed in the middle of the night. It's not becoming." I wanted to say these things were self-evident, but Archibald didn't play the Dictionary Game and there was only so much I could expect from a regular friend.

The closer we got to the kitchen, the clearer the muffled voices became. There were at least three of them. I could make out Nan's and Mrs. Willoughby's, but the third threw me. "Who's that?" I whispered.

Archibald didn't say anything, but she wasn't singing Jesus songs, so I crossed witches off my list. The closer we got to the voices the more Archibald hesitated. "It's going to be all right," I said. "If we stick together." I tugged a little on her hand, and she tucked in beside me. Inch by inch we made our way to the kitchen. It was empty, but we could see through the window into the porch where Nan, in a strange housecoat, was standing next to Archibald's mother. The shape of them had a sadness about it, and I wasn't sure I wanted to get any closer, but Archibald let go of my hand and stepped out on her own. She'd done this before, I could tell.

Archibald joined Nan and Mrs. Willoughby, changing the shape. If it was sad before, it now reached out and touched despair. Mrs. Willoughby didn't scold Archibald or tell her to go back to bed. Instead, her hand fell on her daughter's head, combing her loose curls with her fingers. I stayed where I was. I didn't need to be any closer. The little hairs on my body rose, letting me know they were around, and I wasn't alone.

An RCMP officer stood between the open front door and the rest of us. He shifted from one foot to the other, looking anywhere but at Mrs. Willoughby. "Sorry, Ma'am," he kept saying over and over. I wanted to reach out and apologize to Archibald. I had told her it would be all right, that everything would be okay. That we could sail on my sailboat bed and lie in the hot African sun and not have a care in the world. How was I to know?

I don't know how long we all stood there. The sky cleared, and pink peeked over the horizon. Nan's shushing noises quieted and Mrs. Willoughby was left mumbling on her own. For every "I'm sorry" the officer offered, Mrs. Willoughby countered with a "he promised." Eventually her knees gave way and the RCMP officer and Nan carted her off to the davenport. She lay there with her arm over her eyes, not saying anything at all. Archibald stared down at her, a hard look on her face, like a piece of gum under a school desk.

Nan and the hired girl made arrangements for Mrs. Willoughby's mother to come and see to the children. Nan and I changed back into our rain-soaked clothes. They were still warm from the dryer, but still I was chilled to the bone by the time we tiptoed out of there.

The only good thing was the RCMP officer was waiting for us in the driveway. He didn't say anything when Nan and I slipped onto the front seat beside him, just nodded at Nan. She pulled me on her knee and smelled my hair. "I'll explain later," she said, a little creak in her voice.

I nodded and leaned into her, but she didn't need to explain. I already knew Mr. Willoughby was dead. He'd be buried with the long line of other Messrs., and Mrs. Willoughby would be left to attend his grave alongside theirs. Planting his favourite spring flowers and blooming bushes, brushing aside dead leaves and shoveling away the drifts of snow. Nan said it was a cruel trick to play upon such a young bride.

With a deep sigh she turned and looked straight ahead. I couldn't help but spy a look over my shoulder to make sure one of my should-have-beens wasn't shackled in the backseat. It was a relief that it was empty, but there was always the trunk. I considered asking the officer to open it, but knew Nan's nerves weren't up for any of my shenanigans.

The trip home was quiet, everything fresh-looking from the midnight rain. That's when I started to get a little nervous. I hadn't seen Oswald Elliot since the night before, when he was lit up by the big lightning flash. He was likely sketching something that would make Nan come out of her skin.

We were almost back at Nan's when a thought popped into my mind. No matter what I did, it picked at me and picked at me until it was snapping out of my fingertips. The car's dashboard had a lot of little lights and buttons, and it was just a matter of finding the right one. Before Nan could stop me, I flipped a switch and leaned back.

Sirens.

CHAPTER 26

OSWALD ELLIOT WAS in the hospital for a week after sneaking through Farmer Hempel's cow pasture. A touch of pneumonia is what Doc Marley said. That pencil scratcher missed both the death of Mr. Willoughby and the birth of the man's only child. Nan said it was the only good thing that had happened of late.

Me, Nan, and Old Lady Griggs spoke in whispers as we trudged out of the graveyard and back to the church. I didn't remember the funerals of any of Archibald's other fathers, probably because Mr. Willoughby's was the first I attended. It was hard to watch Archibald cling to her mother with all her other siblings with mix-matched names. They were like a copse of leafless trees, trembling together.

In the church basement long tables had been set up for lunch, and everybody who had stood quiet and dazed were now laughing and talking like the worst part was over. Me and Archibald loaded our plates with pickles and egg salad sandwiches before joining Nan, Old Lady Griggs and her husband, who had been propped up in a chair, saving our spots.

"Can't even lift a pencil let alone make his rounds on his banana-seat bike," Old Lady Griggs was saying as we took two chairs across from her. "The press is at a standstill."

"Are you talking about Oswald?" I said. "Archibald says he's on a hiatus."

Archibald nodded before taking a big bite of her sandwich.

"If it were only that easy," Nan said, handing Archibald a napkin as egg salad oozed out the corners of her mouth.

"A hiatus on *The Canterberry Tales*, but not on *The Deadman's Wife*. Oswald always switches from one strip to the other when there's a —" she looked at us girls, "situation."

"You mean when one of my fathers dies," Archibald said.

"That's right," Griggs said. "But it's only for a month or so, and then he's back on Canterberry. At the moment though he's writing neither, weak as a kitten."

"All the better," Nan said, sliding a plate of cookies across the table. "That man is more interested in sticking his nose in everyone's business than he is in getting his facts right."

"Facts aren't the most important part of the story. They lay the foundation but it's what's built on that foundation that sets the tale apart."

"You do have a way with words, Dorigen."

"I know." Griggs clicked her tongue. "A curse rather than a blessing, I tell you that, Molly. But I've borne it all these years without a complaint. Was telling Mayor Forde about it no more than an hour ago. Told him, while Oswald is on the mend, I can take his place. Even showed him my scrapbook."

Nan ran her teeth over her lip, and Archibald and me sat a little straighter in our seats. "What did he say?" Nan asked.

"The good mayor said a woman cannot be a licensed cartoon journalist."

"What did you say?"

"I said there was no such thing as a licensed cartoon journalist. And he said exactly. He said he told the Whitfords not to sell me coloured pencil crayons. And I've been nothing but a thorn in his side ever since." Griggs picked up a cookie and waved it through the air. "That's what I wanted to talk to you about. I need you to speak to him."

"I don't think we need to get into that here." Nan scanned the room to see who was listening. She seemed to have forgotten me and Archibald.

"No one cares." Griggs' lazy eye wobbled.

"I do, and I don't want to be a part of it."

"You are a part of it whether you like it or not. If you told Mayor Forde that you'll sue the paper unless I'm in charge of Celia's comic strip, he'd have no choice but let me."

"Nan never sues," I said.

"Neither does my mom," Archibald said.

"Mayor Forde doesn't know that. If the three of us got together — your mother," she pointed at Archibald, "you," a nod towards Nan, "and me — we could stir things up." Griggs finished her cookie and patted Nan's hand with her crumby fingers. "To be honest, things have changed so much since Celia started coming over. I don't have to say a word now; folks look at me as if I know things. Walking down Main Street in my honeymoon hat, with my head held high, everybody gives me a wide berth. Tipping their hats, waving at me with their white-gloved hands." She waved right there at the table, as if she were seeing it in her mind's eye. "I think people are scared, like if I had a mind to I could sic Celia on them, same as Walter Douglas does his cat. I don't know why, though I might have made reference to something like that in passing."

Griggs put a straw in her husband's cup and lifted it to his sewn-on lips. "A little throwaway remark I didn't think anyone would take seriously. And now, lo and behold, here I am sitting here with all three of you, thicker than thieves. We could call ourselves the Scrapbook Conspirators. Wouldn't that be lovely?" Griggs set down her husband's cup and grinned. "Birds of a feather."

CHAPTER 27

NOT LONG AFTER, toward the end of August, Nan and Old Lady Griggs opened the black scrapbook together. We sat side by side on Griggs' plastic-covered chesterfield as if it were an everyday occurrence. "You've been asking about your should-have-been grandfather," Griggs said. "And your Nan's honeymoon hat."

I wasn't sure what to say. Nan never talked about her man, and I could see it in her eyes she didn't really want to talk about him now.

"I've always been afraid that someone would tell you," Nan squeezed my hand. "And I think it's best you hear it from me." Her gaze flickered to Griggs. "I mean, us."

Griggs slipped the book from her lap to Nan's. Nan's wrinkled hand patted the dusty cover. "I can't do this," she said after a time. "I really can't, I thought I could, but I can't." She slid the book back to Griggs before she got up to leave. "You'll have to, Dorigen."

For the first time since Griggs and I had shared scrapbook stories, it looked like she was going to cry. There was no glee in her fingertips as she flipped open the book and ran a finger along the strips. It took her some time before she found what she was looking for. "Here it is," she said. "The origin story. Oswald drew it long after it happened, and everything he wrote here is only rumour; your Nan never spoke of it. Not even to me." She took a deep breath and began to read.

The Case of the Midnight Drifter. Griggs read in her regular voice, no flourishes or stretched out elocutions. She read it as if it were a eulogy, and the drawings weren't coloured or shaded in with her pencil crayons. In the first frame, Nan was young, thin and twirling around the kitchen to some song on the radio. She was barefoot, no hard-soled shoes. The next frame held a man, skulking around the outside of her house like some kind of hunchbacked shadowy drooler. I gasped when I saw him. The kind of midnight killer that could carve something in a little girl's headboard. Griggs patted my leg, her lazy eye so still and fixed that it could have been paralyzed.

In the next frame the screen on the door was slashed. The music stopped playing, and Nan stopped dancing. I don't think she's danced in the kitchen since. Not once. Not even when I sang the lead part from La Traviata. But seeing that I don't speak Italian, don't know any of the songs or what it's about, I can understand why she wasn't inspired, even though she said she loved it.

The sadness on young Nan's face made it hard to breathe. I didn't want to know about my should-have-been grandfather anymore, and I was sorry I'd even asked. When I looked at the next frame all I saw was my Nan lying on the kitchen floor, her face all bruised. She was weeping and trying to cover herself with her torn dress. The should-have-been's shadow was long gone. And she was left all alone, except for Walter Douglas, who was laying his elbow-patched sweater over her shoulders and looking back towards the screen door banging in the wind. A wild look was on his face.

I looked from the scrapbook page to Griggs. She closed the book and I knew I would never look forward to sifting through its pages again.

"It's hard to understand," Griggs said. "And no one expects you to, but I think it's answered most of your questions."

I nodded and slipped off the chesterfield to go find my Nan.

CHAPTER 28

THE NEXT MORNING I eyed Nan at the breakfast table. She was biting her lip and turning over an unopened letter. She was so preoccupied that I was able to put three handfuls of brown sugar on my Corn Flakes before she caught on.

"Celia, that's enough."

I put my hand back into the sugar bag and grabbed another handful. She didn't even blink. It was kind of our thing; Nan pretending to be cross and me pretending to be sorry. The milk in my bowl was now a lovely brown colour. I licked my lips as my spoon scooped up that first delicious mouthful. "Nan, aren't you going to open that?"

Nan frowned. "Not now, Celia." She set the letter against a mason jar full of fresh-cut sweet peas.

"Why not?"

"No reason." She took a sip of coffee and turned towards the window.

I took another bite of the brown sugary goodness. "I was thinking if Griggs drew for the Happy Valley Journal I could have a normal kid head."

Nan didn't say anything.

"And Mrs. Whitford could be arrested for beaning baby animals with her trotters."

We hadn't talked about the comic strip since Griggs had shown me my should-have-been grandpa. Nan's lip twitched and I knew she wanted to say something. I was pretty sure it was probably about Mrs. Whitford. The thought of her trying to tie her owl children's shoes with her pink cloven feet could mesmerize us for hours.

Nan didn't talk about any of those things. Instead, she said, "Hurry up. It's going to take a month of Sundays to get the sugar out of your system."

The layer of thick brown goodness at the bottom of my bowl looked like Christmas. I was licking my lips when Nan snatched my bowl away. "Let's get out to the garden," she said. "Before the day gets away on us."

"Yes ma'am," I said, feeling more disappointment than the time Billy Billboson wouldn't let me join the European Cheese Tasters. Kind of made me annoyed, since it was a prerequisite for the PIS ladies. Even though the boys weren't girls, their mothers had been willing to make an exception, especially because Billy looked particularly striking in purple. "But I was actually thinking about doing something else."

"Like what?"

I shrugged.

"Well until you figure it out, we'll spend the morning in the garden."

I wanted to tell her I didn't feel like Anna Karenina this morning and the thought of gardening as anyone else was unacceptable, but I knew Nan wouldn't take me seriously. She'd roll her eyes and say, "Honestly, Celia, some days."

In spite of my misgivings I trudged outside in my Russian rubber boots. The sun was rather hot for so early in the morning, and I was worried it might be too much for my delicate skin.

When I brought it up to Nan, she said I was being ridiculous and refused to carry an umbrella to shade me. I had to pick peas without tearing the whole plant out of the ground, which I was mostly successful at. I only had to replant five when Nan wasn't looking. But the worst were the raspberry bushes with those tiny thorns; they deliberately pricked the ends of my tender digits. If we ever got a harpsichord I couldn't imagine playing it, not now after I'd been so damaged.

When we finally went into the house for lunch I understood why so many Russians hated gardening and preferred long division. But instead of making us something to eat, like she usually did, Nan stared at the letter. The same one she'd turned over and over at breakfast.

"Who's it from?" I asked.

"Your mother," Nan said, a little bit of a robot in her voice.

I felt my heart flip-flop. "My should-have-been ma?" The thought of my mother writing a letter seemed as unnatural as Tiberius taking up ballet: both activities were far too refined for the participants. "What's it say?"

"I don't know, haven't opened it." Nan set it back against the mason jar. "It can keep," she said, as she got out a can of salmon for sandwiches. As we ate we both stared at that letter, as if just looking was enough to make us burst into flames.

We stared at that letter for three more days. Then I accidentally mentioned it to Griggs. Once Griggs got wind of it, she wouldn't let it go. "You know, Molly, I'm not one to put my nose where it doesn't belong."

Nan grunted.

"But this time I'll make an exception." Griggs pursed her lips as if she were about to say something profound. "That letter could be about nothing or it could be life-changing."

"How could anything Audrey has to say be life changing?"

Audrey — my should-have-been ma's name. The way Nan

said it, it sounded all cut-crust sandwiches and bubble baths. But I knew better, I'd seen her greasy, grimy hair, and I knew none of it was true.

Nan looked from me to Griggs and slowly ripped open the envelope. Her face turned pale and all her wrinkles sagged to the bottom.

"What's it say, Molly?"

Nan didn't say anything. Her empty eyes looked through me. She didn't even notice when I put both elbows on the table. Never even said *Mable, Mable, strong and able, get your elbows off the table.* I loved it when she said that, especially the part about the horses stable. When she said that part I'd tell her that the baby Jesus was born in a stable, and if he could put his elbows on the table it wasn't bad manners, it was godly. Nan never said anything to that; instead she'd raise an eyebrow and I'd move my elbows.

I wasn't moving my elbows now. I slid them farther on the table, until I was almost lying flat out on top of it. From there I wasn't going to miss anything. I looked from Nan to Griggs. The old lady was filling with impatience, and it would be only a matter of time until it got the best of her. I began to count. I'd barely gotten to ten steamboats when Griggs snatched the letter from Nan's hand. "If you're not going to read it, I will."

Nan reach for the page but pulled her hand back. "Maybe you're right."

As Griggs unfolded the letter it felt like old times, except this time I was sprawled out on the kitchen table and not stuck to the plastic-covered chesterfield. "Can you use your Agnes Obermeyer voice?" I asked. "I think it suits my should-have-been."

Griggs tilted her head to one side. "You may be right there, but a hint of Whitford would make it more authentic."

I nodded.

She cleared her throat and began to read. If the letter hadn't been so nasty it would have been magical.

Let me make this short and sweet. Since it has come to my attention that Happy Valley is planning to use Celia as a cash cow, I want my take. It's only fair. And considering I have never signed away my parental rights, and neither has my man, it's time to make things legal. We will give Celia over to you, if you give your house over to us, or sell it and give us the proceeds. We expect an answer by the end of the week.

"That's it?" I asked, flummoxed.

Griggs turned the paper over. "Yup, it's not even signed. A signature would require more energy than your should-have-been was willing to spare."

"Are you sure it's from her?" I asked.

Nan took the letter back. "I'm sure," she said. "I'd recognize that handwriting anywhere."

Griggs lifted my chin with a finger. "Put on your long-sleeved shirt, Celia. If that cat wants a fight, we'll give her one."

CHAPTER 29

THE FIGHT we gave my should-have-been wasn't really much of a fight at all. Nan packed two suitcases and we headed over to Griggs' house. Nan said if Audrey wanted the house she could have it; she'd keep me. She said I was the better part of the bargain. "Molly," Old Lady Griggs said as she poured Mr. Griggs' morning coffee, "I wouldn't be in such a hurry to give away the farm. That girl doesn't have a leg to stand on."

"That may well be, but I'm not taking any chances." Nan ran her fingers through my uncombed hair until they got stuck in the sticky bits from dinner last night. She pulled her hand away and wiped it on Griggs' wrinkled table cloth. "I don't want Celia to spend any more time with those two than she already has."

I nodded.

"Well you can live here as long as you want," Griggs said, patting the back of Mr. Griggs' hand. "We won't even charge too much rent."

Nan turned pale. "I don't know how long I can sleep on a plastic-covered chesterfield."

"You'll get used to it. I sleep on a plastic-covered bed."

Nan walked out of the room without saying another word.

It took almost a week before an auction could be arranged. At first Nan said I couldn't come; she said it was a dirty business and she didn't want me anywhere near it. But after Griggs spent most of the morning yelling at Mr. Griggs because he refused to watch me — he wouldn't even nod his head to acknowledge me standing there — Nan said she didn't want to be the cause of any more marital discord. She took me by the hand and whisked me out of the house faster than I could say Jack Robinson. We could still hear Griggs yelling when we got to Nan's house. My should-have-been pa's truck was sputtering in the dirt driveway. I scanned the ground for mud puddles. There were none, and no earthworms to wrap around steering wheels. It was a sign. Now he could never be a banker or rodeo clown.

Nan's hand trembled overtop mine. "Never thought I'd see the day," she started, but couldn't finish. I wanted to ask her what day, but just then out of the corner of my eye I caught sight of Archibald Frankenstein-walking towards me. I ripped my hand from Nan's and adjusted my bolty neck. I stiff-legged it through the throng. This was going to be the best house auction ever. Most of The Ladies of the Perpetual Indigence Society were there. They'd brought their own lawn chairs so they could sit in the shade and cool themselves with paper fans. Mrs. Whitford had yet to arrive; she was probably planning on making some kind of statement.

I noted that most of my first grade class was there. Even Miss Dobbs showed up, luckily for me she was standing downwind. Oswald Elliot was keeping downwind of her as well. I didn't blame him, after their failed parking lot romance. It must have almost killed him, being locked in a car on a hot summer's evening, kissing a pee-soaked teacher.

Archibald and me met in the midst of that marvellous mayhem. "Archibald," I said, "Fancy meeting you here."

She Frankenstein-curtsied. "It's almost as good as our spiderweb and dust bunny circus."

"Almost," I said squeezing her hand. "Except this time Nan is going to lose her house."

Archibald blew out her cheeks. "I didn't think of that."

"Yeah, it's almost killing her to live with Old Lady Griggs. The two of them are always arguing over who should do the cooking. Nan says she'd like to live to see her next birthday and Griggs counters with 'birthdays are overrated.' Nan says Griggs makes her point for her. That's when I leave the kitchen."

Archibald's eyes widened. Since our sleepover, she'd found Nan frightening, and I think the thought of her and Griggs together made Archibald quake in her boots. She turned from me and looked at Nan's old two-story house. "What are you going to do when it sells?"

I shrugged. I hadn't thought that far ahead, but with all the folks wandering around the yard, poking their fingers into this and measuring that, it was bound to be gone by the end of the day. The place was bursting at the seams. Nan never had that many people over on purpose. They didn't mind the flowerbeds or stay on the walking paths the way Nan liked. It was like a bunch of cattle having a free-for-all. For the first time since the letter, a queasiness washed over me. And just when I thought the darkness was going to overtake me, I spied Griggs sticking out her tongue at Oswald. I smiled at Archibald, and we hightailed it in their direction.

"You can hardly hold a pencil," Griggs said. "How do you expect to do justice to a momentous event such as this?"

Oswald licked his pencil lead and walked away. Archibald

and me followed, encouraging Griggs to let it all out. "He's never even drawn Mrs. Whitford with trotters," I said. "Let alone tornado hair."

Griggs nodded and jutted her chin out farther.

"And what about all your great voice work? Has anyone even acknowledged that? First the comic strip then maybe the CBC. Mr. Griggs would come out of his skin. Pour you a morning coffee."

She lit up and got between Oswald and his destination, with Archibald and me flanking him. All the years of colouring Oswald's renderings had been too much for her, and she couldn't help but let her resentment spill out.

"You are never going to win the Pulitzer Surprise without my help."

Archibald and me were on our tiptoes. "What else, Griggs?" I encouraged her, not wanting her to leave anything out.

"Look at me, you plucked pigeon! I'm your best chance."

Oswald didn't say anything. He just stared at his sketchpad, pushing down hard on his pencil until the lead broke under the pressure.

Agnes Obermeyer sidled up beside us. "Are you harassing the intrepid Oswald Elliot?"

"Of course," Griggs snapped. "What else would I do on a day as fine as this?"

"Mind if I join you?" Agnes was in her outdoor bedroom slippers. The ones with the dried clumps of mud infused into the plush purple fuzz. "If anyone needs harassing it's Oswald Elliot. He mocks me in front of the God-appointed mayor."

"Leave me alone." Oswald's lip quivered. "I'm not answering to the likes of you two regarding my artistic merit."

"Oh, I don't need you to answer to me," Agnes said. "I'm here to supervise, on orders from the mayor." Her cigarette bobbed between her parched lips. "Write that down."

"I'm not writing down anything you say." Oswald's voice cracked. "Not everything you utter is a proclamation."

"It should be."

The four of us followed that gangly pencil-scratcher for most of the afternoon. He tried to give us the slip, but we divided and conquered, capturing him in a pincer move. I tried to get Griggs and Agnes Obermeyer to Frankenstein-walk with Archibald and me, but they wouldn't hear of it; Agnes said she couldn't in her fluffy outdoor slippers, and Griggs said she wasn't of the mind to endure more than her usual amount of public humiliation.

I was so caught up with ganging up on Oswald Elliot that I completely forgot about my should-have-beens. It wasn't until I Frankenstein-walked past the rusty grey truck I remembered they were somewhere about, waiting for the auctioneer to drop his gavel and declare them rich. My fingers tingled the way they always did when I was tempted to do something I shouldn't. I leaned over and whispered in Archibald's ear. "Want to go find my should-have-beens?"

Archibald straightened her bolty neck and blinked. "Is that a good idea?"

"Probably not."

"Okay."

Slipping away from Griggs and Agnes was easy. They were so focused on Oswald Elliot we could have set off firecrackers between their toes and they wouldn't have noticed. It was Nan that I had to be on the lookout for. She'd never let me within grabbing distance of the should-have-beens.

Archibald and me stopped our Frankenstein-walking because it attracted too much attention, and we became Robin Hood and Maid Marian. We were in Sherwood Forest, slipping in between the trees, masquerading as people. It took some searching, but while most were distracted by the arrival of Mrs.

Whitford, the Sheriff of Nottingham, in her new bright red convertible car, I spied them leaning against Nan's clothesline pole, my should-have-been ma on one side and my should-have-been pa on the other. I gasped. Besides looking so casual, smirking like a game had been won, my should-have-been ma was wearing Nan's peacock scarf.

Archibald tapped me on the shoulder and pointed. I nodded. We dropped to our bellies and slithered a little closer. Mayor Forde stepped over us as he made a beeline to the clothesline. He stuck out his hand and introduced himself. It was hard to hear what exactly they were talking about, so Archibald and me did one more slither. "Mayor Forde," I snaked-hissed as we made our way closer, "keeps a small rodent in his belly button hole."

Archibald stopped slithering. "He does?"

I nodded. "At town council meetings it pops out whenever he needs an extra pair of hands. That's why he's the God-appointed mayor."

"I wondered," she said, and slithered on.

A feeling of relief ran through me. Now I wouldn't be the only one eye-spying the mayor's navel, trying to see if anything poked out of his shirt's buttonhole loops. And Nan would be hard-pressed to call Archibald, newly orphaned again, rude. Especially if I said it was Archibald's idea. In my mind I could hear Nan clicking her tongue and saying, "If it makes the orphan girl happy, who am I to stand in the way?"

When we were within earshot we heard Mayor Forde ask, "You've signed the papers?"

"We did." My should-have-been pa chewed the inside of his cheek.

"That's a relief." The mayor wiped his dripping brow with a hanky.

"For who?" My should-have-been pa looked suspicious.

Mayor Forde didn't say anything.

"Well let's get it over with." My should-have-been pa had the same look on his face he'd had when he was asking after Nan's hiding place.

"Be patient," Mayor Forde said. "There is a time and place for everything. First the three-legged races, and then the auction."

When Archibald heard the words *three-legged races* she forgot that we were supposed to be invisible and squealed. "We could Frankenstein-walk it!"

"We could," I said, torn between spying and Frankenstein-racing with Archibald.

My should-have-been pa hollered at the mayor, "What kind of shithole town has Sunday races at a house auction?"

"The kind," Mayor Forde said, "that wants all the stragglers to have time to arrive. The more stragglers, the more cash."

My should-have-been pa spat on the ground before nodding. For more cash he could wait.

After the potato sack races and egg toss, the auctioneer brought down his gavel. "Let's get this auction started," he said. "I have a funeral in the next county in an hour. The widow is anxious to move on. Wants to sell the farm while the family's down."

There was a bit of a mumbling — I wasn't sure if it was disapproval or admiration — and a bit of jostling as everyone found their spots. Archibald and me climbed into the back seat of the Whitford's convertible. It had been parked on the front lawn, close to the auctioneer's platform. Mrs. Whitford didn't notice; she was too busy looking down her nose at Agnes Obermeyer. Lucky for me, I had a lot of mud to pick off the bottoms of my bare feet. I'd taken my shoes off to do some earthworm saving with Archibald, having to wade in some puddles past my ankles. Once my soles were picked clean, it was a delight to run them through the plushy, convertible floor carpet.

Before the auctioneer even called for a bid, Mr. Douglas walked up, unpinned a line of medals from his shirt, and handed them to the auctioneer. I'd never seem them before; I didn't even know Mr. Douglas had them. At first the auctioneer looked confused, but then his face lit up. "Folks," he said. "Here we have our first bid. It's a bit unconventional, but this whole situation is." He held up the medals for the crowd to admire. "A man had to go to hell and back to be awarded these." He looked at Mr. Douglas. "Is this your bid?"

Mr. Douglas nodded.

The auctioneer, after consulting with the mayor, accepted the bid.

My should-have-been pa pulled away from the clothesline. "What kind of shit show is this?"

Mayor Forde shrugged. "The Happy Valley kind."

The auctioneer called out, "Any other bids?"

Agnes Obermeyer offered her favourite pair of fluffy slippers but they were quickly rejected. Mrs. Whitford was the only one who offered cash, but Mr. Whitford made her take it back. How could a handful of bills compete with war medals? But it was Old Lady Griggs who won the day. She gave the auctioneer two mismatched buttons.

He held them up. "This is your bid?" he asked, incredulous. Griggs looked almost as regal as the queen. "It is."

"Two buttons for a house?"

She nodded. "And I think it's a generous bid at that."

The PIS ladies dissolved into uncomfortable giggles. Oswald Elliot stepped forward. It was his turn to taunt. "Get them from the bottom of your purse, Mrs. Griggs?"

She gave him her most imperious smile. "Of course not. Don't be ridiculous. They're Mr. Griggs' eyes. Giving up his sight, for our little Celia, he is. Can't imagine a greater sacrifice, can you?"

There was a gasp, and then the auctioneer brought down his gavel. "Sold."

———

Griggs didn't let Nan forget her husband's noble deed. Mr. Griggs wore dark sunglasses with black threads hanging under them. It came up every time she came over for tea.

"We can sew on other buttons," Nan said while pouring.

"He doesn't want other buttons. He's made the sacrifice for your benefit, and I think it's sacrilege for you to dismiss it with such ease."

"I'm not dismissing anything." Nan paused and inhaled deeply. "But I think claiming *sacrilege* is a stretch."

"You prefer blasphemy?"

They were playing the dictionary game. I almost squealed in delight.

"That's a little irreverent." Nan offered Griggs cream and sugar. From under the table, I heard the little spoons swirling in their cups as I watched Nan's rotating ankle and Griggs' pulsating vein. I patted my dust bunny, everything was as it should be.

Thanks for reading *Canterberry Tales*. If you enjoyed this book, a review would be much appreciated as it helps other readers discover the story.

If you haven't joined my email list please do. You'll get access to all of my new releases at bargain basement prices before they are available anywhere else. Thanks again.

All my best,
C.P. Hoff
Join my email list:
www.cphoff.com/sign-up

ALSO BY C. P. HOFF

The Picaresque Narratives

West of Ireland

A Town Called Forget

The Happy Valley Chronicles

Canterberry Tales

A Crack in the Teacup

A peek at Celia's next adventure
A Crack in the Teacup

A Crack in the Teacup
C.P. Hoff

"I don't think Captain Ahab would approve," I said, leaning on the ironing board. "Sailors never starch, it's against the rules. Besides Queegueg chafes."

Nan rolled her eyes. She'd stopped caring about Captain Ahab's opinion the day my best friend Archibald and me played on my sailboat bed and tried to harpoon her with sharpened willow sticks. Nan was furious. I'd never seen her that mad for such a petty thing. But when it came right down to it, it was her fault. She was the one who insisted on reading me the classics. She could have read me *Hop on Pop* or *Danny and the Dinosaur*, like the sensible parents of the kids in my class, but she said she'd rather gouge out her eyes with a spoon.

I remember the first time I traced a finger over the embossed letters on her copy of *Moby Dick*. They rose and fell under my touch like little waves. When Nan cleared her throat and read the words 'Call me Ishmael,' I almost gasped. Who wouldn't want to be called Ishmael? But that wasn't the only discovery I made. A whole raft of hard-nosed brutes swaggered between those pages.

Nan's regular book-reading voice was almost as good as Old Lady Griggs' comic-strip-reading one. Except Nan didn't have a plastic-covered chesterfield, so I could listen without worrying about my skin peeling off when I stood up. Griggs and I became thick as thieves last summer when Nan took a job at the druggist's and had her look after me. That's how I learned that Oswald Elliot, Happy Valley's newspaperman, had created a comic strip starring yours truly, detailing my exploits after my should-have-been parents abandoned me at the hospital maternity ward. My very existence was a scandal in town, and Griggs was the one who showed me just how infamous I was.

When Nan got to Queequeg, shivers ran down my spine. I knew I'd never have a braver storybook friend, that he'd accompany me anywhere I wanted to go and never breathe a word of it. Despite all his attributes, though, Nan's lips tightened whenever I brought him up. The harpooning incident had soured her on him for good.

The more I talked of Queequeg chafing, the more Nan starched. She should have known that trying to make me look perfect on the first day of second grade wouldn't make any difference. All the moms dropping off kids would still sniff and turn their backs on me, and the kids—those that didn't have spitballs at the ready—would thumb their noses and run to tell a teacher things I hadn't even thought about doing yet. Besides, who was Nan to judge my appearance, standing in the middle of the kitchen in her housecoat and curlers? She wasn't even wearing any support garments.

"Celia," she said, brandishing the iron, "try to keep clean for at least five minutes."

I spritzed the iron to make it hiss. "Which five? The first or the last? Cause if it's the first, that's easy. Even Queequeg could do that. He could do it with his eyes closed. But if it's the last five minutes, you might as well ask for the moon."

Nan's nostrils pinched together as she handed me my crisp white shirt. "Sometimes, child, you try my patience."

I spritzed once more for good measure. "Sometimes?" I sighed, knowing Nan wasn't being entirely truthful.

Nan turned and headed upstairs, and I padded after her. With all the starching, we were a little behind schedule, and if we didn't hurry, we'd miss the first bell. I wanted to tell Nan she should be more organized, but she'd only blame me. Say that if I hadn't used my new cotton shirt as an earthworm way station

CHAPTER ONE

she wouldn't have spent half the night bleaching and scrubbing out the marks.

I huffed out all the exasperation that was building in me as I pulled back the sail on my sailboat bed. A brand new pink plaid suspender skirt was waiting for me on the bedspread. I ran a finger over the criss-crosses. Nan had ordered it from the Simpsons-Sears catalog. It didn't look as special on my bed as it had on the girl with the staple through her cheek, all twirly and innocent. Nan and her wishful thinking.

Next to the skirt was a pair of white knee socks. Coupled with the starched shirt I was holding, it was a cute and unassuming ensemble. I hoped it might lull my new teacher into letting down her guard. It was an admirable plan, if not a lofty one.

All summer long, worry about my new teacher had been bubbling in the back of my mind, when I wasn't saving earthworms or burying one of Archibald's dads. (Archibald's mom had a string of unlucky husbands. Old Lady Griggs said they were lightning rods when it came to attracting peculiar deaths, like they were in a competition to get in the book of Guinness World Records. Oswald Elliot wrote a comic strip about Archibald and her assorted fathers too. I was a bit jealous when I found out, but I got over it.)

What if my new teacher was like my old one, Miss Dobbs, who was boy-crazy for Oswald Elliot (yuck) and smelled like pee? (Double-yuck.) What if she sat in the staffroom with the other teachers, chain-smoking cigarettes and laying bets on which child would be the first to hear the words *turn to your left* in a police lineup? For teachers, that was as fun as shooting craps. And worse than that, what if my new teacher made me sit in the front row where she could whack me with her yardstick?

When I'd fastened my last suspender button, I ventured into Nan's room. She was examining herself in her bureau mirror. She was wearing the same outfit she'd worn on my first day of grade one: the forest green and florescent pink Fortrel sheath dress. I flopped down on her bed, as casual as can be. "We'll walk slow," I said, picking at her tufted chenille bedspread. "Wouldn't want anything to bust loose."

Nan stood on her toes to examine herself more thoroughly. Her brow furrowed, and I knew what she was thinking. After the debacle with my should-have-been parents last summer— the derelicts who tried to blackmail Nan into giving up her house—Nan took to calisthenics and brisk walks. She said the younger she stayed, the easier it would be to keep disaster at bay. Even Old Lady Griggs noticed that Nan had firmed up a fair amount. Said Nan would waste away if she dropped another twenty-five pounds. She was right; Nan looked better in that sheath dress than she had last year, but I couldn't let her know that. I had my reasons.

Nan's laundry business had dwindled to almost nil because of those newfangled automatic washers and tumble dryers everyone was buying, hence her part-time job at the druggist's this summer. Spritzing while she ironed was one of my favourite pastimes, but because I didn't get to do it so much anymore, I took to spritzing Nan when she did her jumping jacks. In one of my spritzing frenzies it occurred to me that if Nan wanted to be more youthful, the age spots had to go. And if bleach worked on my Nan's whitest whites, why not on Nan? I practiced flicking bleach on the back of her forest green and pink Fortrel sheath dress. Where the stuff hadn't burned right through, whiteish, colourless blotches appeared. But to tell Nan that now was inadvisable.

Nan twisted once more in the mirror but couldn't see her full backside. I had no choice; I had to push the point. "Old Lady Griggs said that sometimes old people bloat for no apparent reason."

CHAPTER ONE

"I'm not old." Nan gave her skirt a tug, but I knew she was having second thoughts.

"Have it your way." I shrugged and rolled onto my back. "But don't blame me if there's another Miss Dobbs incident."

By the way Nan's eyes flashed, I saw the seed was sown. Nan made her way to the closet and started shifting the hangers. No one wanted to be like Miss Dobbs, my unfortunate first grade teacher. On the first day of school last year, she slipped in what Timmy Crybaby-Head's mom called "a hallway incident." Everybody else's mom said it was Crybaby-Head's pee. As Miss Dobbs slid along the linoleum floor, her form-fitting pencil skirt split at the seam, exposing her Playtex Living girdle. Nan said the only good thing about the debacle was that it brought her down a couple of pegs.

When Nan finished her primping, we were off. We'd almost made it through the schoolyard when I was overcome. The Happy Valley School for Reluctant Children was right next to the Happy Valley Penitentiary, a bleak monolith of grey stone. Mayor Forde said its proximity was an object lesson for delinquents with sloppy grades, and a cost-saving measure since the side-by-side institutions shared a chain-link fence topped with razor wire.

They added the razor wire to the penitentiary side when Dinky Farmickel hopped the divider to play hopscotch with his niece, Pew Pew Petunia. That got the entire town debating the safety of the schoolchildren, and some even threatened to vote Mayor Forde out of office. Eventually, they decided against it, because Mayor Forde was the *God-appointed* mayor. And since Dinky didn't mean any harm and hadn't flashed any of the children, most folks concluded it was the most thoughtful thing a man could do—play with a shunned child, that is, not break out of the clink. Dinky, who hadn't finished the sixth grade, fit right in, hopscotching in his prison stripes like there was no tomorrow.

Even with the extra razor wire, my knees buckled. I'd promised myself that I wasn't going to look, that I wasn't going to make a thorough search of the prison yard, but with all the men over in the Happy Valley Penitentiary clamouring to wish students luck on the first day of the new school year, I had to see if my should-have-been father was in the mix. I scanned the fenceline with my beady eyes for a scraggily man with butter-covered teeth. He was nowhere in sight. Relief and disappointment filled me in equal measure; relief that he wasn't nearby, and disappointment that he was free as a bird after trying to cheat Nan out of her house.

Nan squeezed my hand, so I knew she was as anxious as I was. We quickened our pace to the door of the Happy Valley School for Reluctant Children. I perused the hall. Archibald had to be somewhere in the free-for-all, it was just a matter of ferreting her out. With Nan so close at hand, yelling was out of the question; she didn't care for raised voices indoors. Without knowing where Timmy Crybaby-Head was piddling, jumping was not advised either. One slip, and all Nan's ironing and starching would be out the window.

That's when I heard a familiar yowl and I knew Archibald was adjusting her bolty neck and getting ready to Frankenstein-walk towards me—our preferred greeting since first grade. I adjusted my own imaginary neck bolt and began dragging my leg behind me. It was only a matter of bouncing off bigger kids until we found each other. It didn't take long. Archibald came drooling and lurching from around Mrs. Hoopenmire, Leonard's mom.

"I'm so glad to see you, Celia," Archibald cried. "It's been a terrible summer for earth worms." She held me in a long embrace.

I nodded. "Yes. It's caused me and Nan no end of worry. Nan says the weather's not fit for man or beast. Old Lady Griggs said if we were smart we'd build an ark."

"I'm with Mrs. Griggs. You know, Queequeg is an excellent sailor."

I wanted to tell Archibald that Queequeg couldn't sail an ark, that arks were for plodding along and blundering into mountains, and Queequeg only had experience maneuvering whaling ships on the high seas, but how could Archibald know? She didn't have a sailboat bed; she'd never fixed her sheets to her curtain rod or braved the waves alongside Captain Ahab. She'd never polished peg legs at midnight either. Worst of all, she didn't have a Nan who read her the classics. Her mother was too busy with Archibald's long line of brothers, and those never-ending funeral arrangements. Considering these things, I let it slide. I had bigger fish to fry.

Looking around the crowded hallway, I spied Miss Dobbs pinching cheeks and patting heads. "I wonder if she still smells like pee," I said, raising an eyebrow.

"Let's go have a sniff." There was more excitement in Archibald's voice than I'd heard in some time. Considering the summer she'd had, I would do anything to make her happy.

Adjusting our bolty necks, we waved goodbye to Nan, and drooled our way towards our first grade teacher.

Miss Dobbs glared at both me and Archibald, which was odd. Usually, she saved her hairy eyeball for me alone.

"You're back," she said, with no love in her voice.

I stepped aside, wondering if her tone would change if only Archibald occupied her sight line.

Miss Dobbs scowled even more.

"That's no way to greet students," I said, stepping back towards Archibald.

"Isn't it?"

CHAPTER ONE

I shook my head. "No. I've been watching. You've been patting heads and pinching cheeks. Aren't we going to get the same treatment?"

A sly smile crossed Miss Dobbs' face as she leaned over and took hold of Archibald's cheek. Archibald winced. "Happy?" Miss Dobbs asked.

I said nothing. Something had happened since first grade to change Miss Dobbs' feelings about Archibald. A year ago, she would have placed Archibald on a feather pillow if she'd had one. Archibald was like Sarah Crewe from *The Little Princess*, and Miss Dobbs the doting Becky. I looked from Miss Dobbs to Archibald. Archibald blinked up at Miss Dobbs as if she was melting inside. I was missing something.

"You're both in the second grade now. You can't expect to be treated like babies any longer."

"We're in Mrs. Carson's class," Archibald said, reaching for my hand.

Miss Dobbs' lips twitched. "Yes, well, there's been a change of plans. Mrs. Carson has spent the better part of the summer at Souris Valley. Doc Marley sent her there after an office misunderstanding. Once she gets out, she'll be in charge of the grade threes. Less medication needed for that bunch, who are more docile than you ragamuffins."

"Oh," I said, a little excited at being called a ragamuffin. "Are we going to be left to our own devices? When Nan takes a bath, she sometimes leaves me to my own devices."

Miss Dobbs went white and looked like she would cry. "I should be so lucky. Principal Wolfe isn't of the same mind. He said since I'm familiar with all the students, and to ease the transition, he's moved me up to the second grade. And those lovely grade ones, the innocents I've looked forward to all summer, get some upstart that has never even swung a yardstick."

CHAPTER ONE

Archibald almost fell over, so I put my arm around her waist to steady her. "That's wonderful," I said, not meaning it.

No matter how I considered my new predicament, there was no upside. The idea of another year with Miss Dobbs made my throat go dry and my lips stick together. I thought back to Griggs and me last summer. The two of us sitting on her plastic covered chesterfield going over how dismal grade one had been. "I'm not sure where it went wrong," I said. "Nan wore her good occasion lipstick on my first day, and told Miss Dobbs that I was an excellent reader and that she wouldn't have any problems in that department. But Miss Dobbs hated me right away.

"She was slipping the last safety pin in the rip of her pencil-peed skirt," I told Griggs, "when she told Nan that she was sure I was amazing, but she'd take over my education from now on. That Nan needn't be troubling herself. All smiles, Miss Dobbs clip-clopped Nan to the door. When the door shut, she rolled her eyes and said, loud enough for all the class to hear, "What does a doddering old spinster know about teaching a child to read?"

I had put my head on Griggs' shoulder at the memory. "I thought all first grade teachers loved their students. Particularly the girls. That they made dandelion chains at recess and played hopscotch before pricking their fingers to become blood sisters."

Griggs sighed. "In a perfect world, that *would* be the case, but this is Happy Valley." She bent over and hauled out the big black scrapbook she kept under her chesterfield. "And disappointment is baked into your back story. There's a good reason Miss Dobbs' doesn't care for you—your mother, Audrey." She flipped through the pages. "Ah. Here it is. The Origins of the Canterberry family. I'm no fan of Oswald Elliot, but he does his research." After a few throat exercises, Griggs began to read an old comic strip I'd never seen before.

Caroline Dobbs is an ordinary child. She walks ordinary,

talks ordinary and sits in her ordinary desk, as any good student should. A teacher's pet in the making. But rosy days aren't on the horizon for poor Caroline Dobbs. Enter stage left, Audrey Canterberry, a wild-eyed girl who's anything but ordinary. She spits, she chews tobacco, and her language—well, this prestigious newsman won't lower himself to print it.

The first time Audrey claps eyes on Caroline, her lip curls up into the most unnatural snarl. "Caroline, teeter-totter with me."

Caroline's eyes widen in horror. "No, thank you."

"I wasn't asking." Grabbing hold of the uncooperative girl, Audrey drags her across the playground to the base of the dreaded apparatus. "Sit," she barks.

Caroline hesitates. To her, a teeter-totter represents splinters and dizzying heights. She can't bear the thought.

Taking a swift jab to the solar plexus, Caroline crumples onto the end of the board and before she has time to recover, is suspended in mid-air by the obstreperous Audrey. "Farmer Brown, Farmer Brown let me down!" Caroline shrieks the international teeter-totter code of submission, but hard-hearted Audrey Canterberry doesn't yield, thumbing her nose at convention. As cool as a cucumber, Audrey examines her nails. "What will you give me if I let you down?"

On the verge of hysterics, Caroline pulls at her once-pristine ponytail. "My lunch? You can have my lunch."

"Got my own."

"My barrettes?" Her hands tremble as she unclips them from her hair.

"Wouldn't be caught dead in butterfly barrettes. Now if they were skull and crossbones, we might have a deal."

"My favourite socks?" She lifts a leg that is not yet shapely.

"I'll pass."

Whatever she offers, it is not enough. Sadly, for Caroline

Dobbs, it is only the first day of her misery. Countless others follow. When a new boy starts school, Audrey wraps him around her little finger before Caroline can get her shoes on. When Caroline wears something special, Audrey spoils it. How long will their rivalry continue? Only time, and the Happy Valley Journal, will tell.

"So you see," Griggs said, closing the scrapbook, "your first day of school wasn't the first time Miss Dobbs laid eyes on you. Not the real you anyway. Oh, she's likely seen you around town, wandering aimlessly, but I doubt that's what's fueled her wrath. Like it or not, you look a bit like your should-have-been ma Audrey, especially around the eyes. How could Caroline Dobbs forget the face of her grade school nemesis?" Griggs leaned back on her plastic covered chesterfield and sighed. "I think Caroline took one look at you and all her school memories came flooding back. And believe you me, none of them were good."

"What did Nan do about Audrey's bullying?"

"Not enough. She was furious, of course. Horrified her daughter would behave in such a way. But try as she might, she couldn't stop her. She warned Audrey, then grounded her, but no matter what she tried, Audrey didn't care. That's why as soon as your Nan found out Caroline was going to be your grade one teacher, she made sure you could read and write. I think she hoped lightening her load would make up for your should-have-been's sins."

But it hadn't. And now Archibald and me were paying the price. Puffing out my cheeks, I looked at Archibald before we both trudged after Miss Dobbs into the classroom with our hearts in our shoes. I didn't know if we'd ever hold hands and swing our arms again.

"At least Miss Dobbs doesn't smell like pee this year," I whispered.

"Not yet," Archibald replied grimly.

CONTENTS

Praise for C.P. Hoff	i
About the Illustrator	iii
The Happy Valley Chronicles	vii
Dear Reader	xi
Chapter 1	1
Chapter 2	12
Chapter 3	18
Chapter 4	30
Chapter 5	40
Chapter 6	58
Chapter 7	66
Chapter 8	72
Chapter 9	80
Chapter 10	90
Chapter 11	98
Chapter 12	106
Chapter 13	110
Chapter 14	120
Chapter 15	124
Chapter 16	134
Chapter 17	148
Chapter 18	158
Chapter 19	168
Chapter 20	174
Chapter 21	186
Chapter 22	198
Chapter 23	202
Chapter 24	212
Chapter 25	222
Chapter 26	228

Chapter 27	234
Chapter 28	238
Chapter 29	244
Dear Reader	253
Also by C. P. Hoff	255
A Crack in the Teacup	257
Chapter One	261

Printed in the USA
CPSIA information can be obtained
at www.ICGtesting.com
JSHW081157310823
47338JS00001B/55